Adrien's sexual adventures

Paul Mail

The beginning of the adventure

In the middle of the morning, Adrien slowly got out of his bed. Since he no longer had to get up early in the morning to take his physiotherapy lessons, each waking up was more and more difficult for him. It had been almost three months since his aunt Viviane had died of a heart attack, bequeathing him all his fortune and he let himself live in his little two-room apartment in the 14th arrondissement of Paris. Three months that he no longer needed to study or work. Three months he could do what he saw fit without being accountable to anyone.

He got up, put on a black joggers and a cat face t-shirt, and walked to the kitchen for breakfast. Tall and slender with a body with bulging abs thanks to the intensive practice of table tennis, Adrien was rather handsome according to his former girlfriends. His light brown hair was curling and Adrien had that twitch of running his hand through his hair whenever he felt embarrassed or didn't know what to do.

Since the death of his parents in a car accident more than ten years ago, he had been raised by his aunt Viviane. When she entered the faculty, she offered him to live in this two-room apartment she owned near Parc Montsouris so that Adrien could become independent and especially leave his large apartment in the 16th arrondissement.

She was really a shrew, Adrien thought to himself, thinking about his aunt.

In a cupboard, he took some cereal and poured himself a black coffee. In a dish, on the counter, he grabbed an apple and bit it down. Since he had inherited from his aunt, he had quit his studies and let himself live until he decided what he was going to be able to do with his life. Almost three months had already passed and Adrien hadn't made any decision yet. At twenty-four, he seemed to have his whole life ahead of him.

Another day that begins, Adrien said to himself, observing through these windows the passers-by who were walking in the street in the grayness of Paris.

Adrien went out less and less, but he did not miss contact with others. On the asphalt, the flow of cars was incessant and on the sidewalks, the pedestrians all walked with a hurry to get to their work.

He had no more constraints.

After breakfast, he went to his living room in front of a small table against the wall which served as his desk and turned on his laptop. He sat down on his wheelchair and logged into the site where he was spending the most time at the moment: Jackie and Michel. He browsed the different videos looking for the one he was going to watch.

The choice was wide, too wide, but Adrien was curious. He watched the video of a young woman enjoying walking naked in the forest, stroking her sex. He then clicked on the video of a mother and daughter engaging in sexual activity together. In the middle of a fellatio session, the mother was unexpectedly joined by her daughter and they began to suck a man who was even more excited. Two other men then joined them to take care of the mother and daughter.

Adrien found this video of a rare perversity. The table on which the girl was lying kept cracking under the blows of the tail that the girl took. Adrien felt the excitement rising in him. He was getting closer to pleasure when someone rang the doorbell.

— No, Adrien said, interrupting himself at the insistence of his visitor.

Angry, he tucked his penis into his jogging pants and went to open it.

On his doorstep, his friend Tony was growing impatient. Adrien had known Tony from the elementary school benches. They had lost sight of each other a few years before meeting, at random, at a night of medical students where Tony had come to pick up future doctors.

Tony was shorter and thinner than Adrien. He had brown hair that he combed into a peak and always wore low-rise jeans with his butt parted and tight t-shirts. He also wore a white one with a V-neck that stopped at the navel, revealing his flat stomach with a piercing.

— I was around and wanted to come see you, Tony said before entering the apartment.

Adrien served his friend a coffee. He no longer took offense at Tony's cavalier ways, for he knew it was his way of hiding his wounds. Longingly, Tony took the mug Adrien handed him.

— Thank you. You at least know how to receive. It's not like the bully I spent part of the night with, Tony said irritably.

— What happened to you ? asked Adrien, used to his friend's heartache.

Tony huffed, but didn't have to be asked to tell his story. The day before, he had met a handsome man in a bar in the swamp and as always, Tony had thought he had found his prince charming when he only had to deal with a bastard.

— He was a little older, handsome as a god and super muscular. He assured me that I was the type of guy he was looking for. After three glasses, he offered to drink a last one at his place.

— I guess you didn't refuse?

— Why would I say no ?

Tony then confided in her their hot moment of love, omitting no details. The man had a tattoo below his right breast, a black beard collar, and a huge cock.

— He fucked me up, my ass hurts too much.

— That'll teach you.

— I would have liked to taste his cum to get to know him better, but he unloaded everything in my ass, said Tony disappointed.

— And after ?

Tony shrugged.

— As usual. As soon as he finished washing his balls, he told me to shoot myself. He didn't even want me to spend the night with him.

A tear glistened in the corner of his eye, but with a quick gesture, the young man made it disappear.

— Why do you always go to bed the first night? asked Adrien.

— I couldn't resist, he was too cute with his bad boy style.

Tony plopped down on the sofa and put his feet on the coffee table. He knew his love life was a disaster, but he could not resign himself to changing the world of his life. He had always been attracted to infrequent boys.

— It would be easier if you agreed to be my boyfriend, Tony said.

Adrien smiles. He had had this discussion hundreds of times with Tony before. He was not gay and did not want to have a long lasting sexual relationship with his best friend, although there had already been some touching and some handjobs and blowjobs between them.

— You will eventually find the rare pearl, assured Adrien.

— I was sure it was him.

— Like everyone you meet as soon as you've had one too many drinks.

For a few seconds Tony brooded over his misfortune before changing the subject.

— And you, what were you doing before I arrived? Did you take a long time to open up?

— Nothing, I was reading.

— You're kidding me, I've never seen you read anything other than your textbooks and even when you had to.

Tony walked over to the computer that had gone to sleep and moved the mouse. The screen lit revealing Jacquie and Michel's site with the video Adrien was watching a few minutes earlier.

— You should stop jerking off alone in front of your screen. I'm sure it's been months since you touched a real girl.

— Not true, protested Adrien.

— With all the money you have, you shouldn't stay in your house. There is no point in being rich to live like this.

Adrien ran his hand through his hair knowing that his friend was right.

— I'm sure your cock is still all swollen in your jogging. You didn't go to the end, am I wrong?

— You came at the worst time.

— Sorry, Tony said before offering to end his case to be forgiven.

At first Adrien refused, but Tony insisted.

— It's been a long time since I sucked you and it will do you good.

— I like to jerk off in the morning.

— You know I'm a great sucker, Tony said, touching her penis through the joggers.

Adrien had not yet disbanded and the hand that was feeling his cock through the fabric of his jogging was becoming more and more enterprising.

— Do not beg, you know I like to suck you.

Adrien nodded. Already in the school yard, Tony was spending his time staring at his cock when he pissed or trying to touch his cock under his shorts when they were sitting side by side on the benches. Adrien had always let him do it out of friendship.

— All right, Adrien agreed, who now wanted his friend to take care of him.

Tony ran his hand through his joggers and saw that he was not wearing underpants. He lowered his jogging pants and invited Adrien to sit on the sofa to take care of him. He spread her legs first, knelt in front of him and observed Adrien's cock.

— What a beautiful cock! I missed her, he said delighted, gently stroking Adrien's cock.

Gently, Tony leaned down and brought Adrien's cock to his mouth. Slowly, he unbuckled her foreskin and gave it a few deft licks, then thrust it whole into his mouth.

Adrien felt the warmth of his friend's mouth around his cock, which gave him an immediate feeling of pleasure and his cock stood up. He knew his friend was good and he was going to make him cum in no time.

Tony started a quick back-and-forth movement with his mouth around Adrien's cock and then worked hard on his penis.

Very quickly, Adrien's long and thin cock became hard and stretched like an I. Erect, Adrien's cock measured seventeen centimeters. Tony once had fun measuring it while he was jerking it off.

Tony put his left hand around Adrien's cock and swung up and down, searching for Adrien's gaze.

— So ? Isn't it better than jerking off to yourself in front of porn? Tony asked.

— It's certain. If you continue like this, it won't be long before you make me cum.

— Why do you think I'm doing this? Tony said smiling.

He then accelerated his manual movement around the sex of his friend while stroking his scholarships, then he resumed sucking vigorously, pulling sighs from Adrien.

— When you're going to enjoy, especially do not hold back. Unload everything in my mouth. I love when you empty yourself in me.

— All right, Adrien said in agony.

Tony then put Adrien's entire cock in his mouth for a few seconds before resuming his piston movement, lingering on his penis.

Adrien closed his eyes and focused on the pleasure his friend was giving him. No girl had ever sucked it so passionately. With an attentive gesture, Tony was also palpating his balls.

Tony continued his movement when he felt a thrill run through Adrien's body. A second later, a stream of hot cum poured into her mouth. Tony didn't release his friend's cock though. He continued to pump it and pull on it to squeeze out all the semen it contained from his penis. He thus collected several streams of cum in his mouth while Adrien let out cries of pleasure.

When Tony was sure Adrien was done ejaculating, he pulled his mouth back, taking all of his friend's cum with him. His mouth was filled with a viscous, whitish liquid. Tony amused himself by mixing it in his mouth before swallowing it all at once.

— Um, that was too good. I love your cum. This is the best I've ever seen, he said, licking his lips.

On the sofa, Adrien was groggy with pleasure. Tony sucked like no one else.

— You're the best, said Adrien before pulling up his jogging pants and touching his hair. His friend had emptied it.

— You want me to jerk you off? Adrien asked to return the favor to his friend.

— I don't have time there. I have an appointment.

— You're sure ?

— Yes in addition, I already ejaculated in my boxers when you came in my mouth. I have my boxers full of semen, I have to lift them before staining my pants.

Without further ado, Tony took off his wet jeans and boxers. With his boxers, he wiped his wet and shaved cock. Tony didn't have a single hair on his body, he was a fan of full hair removal. The cock in the air, he went to wash his penis in the bathroom before putting his pants back on with nothing underneath.

— I left my boxers in your bathroom, can you wash it for me? I will come back to pick it up on occasion.

— No problem. Where should you go

— I have an appointment in a pizzeria for a waiter job. I have to earn my living a little more regularly.

— I'm sure you'll get the job.

— If I have it, would you agree to bugger me to celebrate? Tony asked.

Adrien huffed. Tony was thinking only of that. He had already refused a thousand times to go further with him, but his friend always came back to the charge. Adrien was afraid of damaging their precious friendship if they became more committed to their relationship.

— Try to keep this job a month later, we'll see.

— If I can, you agree to bugger me, Tony enthusiastically.

Adrien shrugged and promised to think about it if Tony was able to.

— You know that I would like to feel your thin and long tail in me. I'm sure she would fit perfectly with my asshole and wouldn't hurt like the big cock from the other nag that night.

Adrien then wondered if he hadn't signed up too quickly: Tony was able to hold his job for a month just to hope to get fucked in the ass.

— What are you going to do? Tony asked.

— I haven't planned much since I left college.

— If I were as rich as you, I would travel. I would love to visit the world.

Adrien had thought about it, but he had never had the chance to leave and his aunt had never taken him with her on these trips around the world. She left him alone in his large apartment with a succession of supervisors, each more unbearable than the next.

— I don't know where I could go or how?

— Get yourself a Sex and Bed. I wanted to register on their site to offer my services, but my application was not accepted. My maid's room was too small by site criteria.

Adrien frowned and looked questioningly at his friend. He didn't see what he was talking about.

— You do not know ? Tony asked. It's a kind of Airbnb, only better. In addition to the bed and breakfast, the host must offer sexual activity. This site is very well known on the darknet. It's not cheap, but it's worth it seems.

— Never heard of it.

Tony wrote down an email address on a piece of paper.

— It'll do you good to get out of your den, Tony said before kissing Adrien on the cheek and leaving the apartment.

Adrien closed the door behind Tony after watching him nodding from behind as he walked away. His friend had a knack for always passing by unexpectedly, but Adrien didn't care, because he liked Tony. He was his oldest friend. Beneath his whimsical air, Tony had an artichoke heart and overflowed with good feelings.

Out of curiosity, Adrien took Tony's paper and connected to the indicated site which looked like the real Airbnb site. As the name suggests, accommodations with gender were offered to travelers. There was something for everyone, although as Tony had said, the accommodation and services seemed rather upscale. The site brought together individuals who had accommodation and who wanted to offer a little more than just a bed and breakfast.

How did Tony get to know this site? Adrien wondered though it didn't matter.

He clicked on the photos and read several advertisements to get an idea of the services offered.

A farmer from Auvergne with big loaves offered to come and stuff it as many times as possible in the straw while tasting Saint Nectaire. She was posing in front of her farm next to a cow, pulling her big chest out of her shirt. She had big blonde pigtails and green plastic boots, but no pants.

A lawyer living in a large villa in the Aveyron offered a room with cover while accepting sodomy, but refusing to practice it. The menu was available.

In the Basque Country, a couple of tanned and muscular surfers welcomed the visitor in a pagoda near the beach with an initiation to kitesurfing and a three-way kiteboarding.

The rates were not cheap, but the reviews left by visitors were glowing. They all seemed to have had an unforgettable time. A traveler said he had spit his mash five times on the farmer from Auvergne who asked for more each time.

I can try, Adrien said to himself.

Adrien continued to leaf through the ads. Three students at the Sorbonne who lived in collocation shared a fourth bedroom or their bed for a particular visit to Paris.

*They're cute, but it wouldn't be out of place to just change the district. Tony would be kidding me*thought Adrien.

He was hesitating about choosing his destination when another ad appeared on the site. A couple in their sixties from Cannes offered accommodation in their large apartment ten minutes from the sea. They offered full board and were open to all sexual activities. The photos of the apartment were nice and the two retirees showed a sympathetic smile even though they were no longer fresh. The service appeared to be of high quality.

What if I went to see the sea? I may still be able to bathe at the beginning of autumn, Adrien said to himself.

He looked at the price: six thousand euros for three days and two nights. It was expensive, but he had the means since his aunt had left him her fortune. After a last hesitation, he clicked and booked his stay.

On to the holidays, rejoices Adrien determined to have fun.

Cannes stay

At the start of the afternoon, Adrien left Cannes station, his backpack slung over his shoulder. After several unplanned stops in the countryside, his train had finally reached its destination three hours late. The air conditioning had broken down during the trip. Upon arrival, it felt like an old, used handkerchief.

For his stay, he had taken some things, several spare boxers, pants and four t-shirts, a swimsuit, a box of condoms and lubricant. On his cell phone, he entered the address of his Sex and Bed in the GPS. It was barely a fifteen minute walk away. He hesitated to go first to see the sea, but the trip had tired him and he wanted to know where he was going to sleep tonight. Tomorrow he would have time to go for a walk, especially since his train journey, if not pleasant, had already allowed him to admire the red rocks of the Estérel massif which flowed into the sea.

With a quiet step, he walked towards the apartment of the sixties. On the way, he took off his jacket. The climate was much milder than in Paris.

A few moments later, he arrived in front of a bourgeois building which must have been an old hotel transformed into an apartment. He rang on the name indicated by the site: Mr. and Mrs. Rouvier and entered the vast hall, the walls of which were covered with mirrors. Taking an old elevator with a gate, he went up to the third floor where a door was ajar on the landing.

When Adrien approached, the two sixties pictured on the site appeared on the doorstep smiling at him. Monsieur wore a charcoal-blue suit with a striped shirt and a dark tie. His white hair was cut short and a thin goatee surrounded his mouth. Large glasses with golden frames were placed on his nose. He had a beautiful presence and one guessed a well-groomed body under his clothes.

Beside him, a woman with cropped salt and pepper hair was smiling. She wore a tapered black dress open on one side revealing her white skin. A large golden necklace hung from her neck and large earrings from her ears. Several voluminous rings adorned her fingers and bright lipstick adorned her mouth. Her dress hugged a body that with age had thickened in the buttocks and stomach, but she remained attractive.

The man greeted Adrien and invited him to enter. His name was Philippe and his wife Annie. They seemed as uncomfortable as Adrien who wondered how his stay was going to be. To break the embarrassment, Philippe offered Adrien to show him the apartment. He led her into a large living room, the floor of which was covered with solid parquet and the walls adorned with large paintings. On the old varnished furniture, many trinkets were placed. Two large sofas were installed around a large television screen mounted on the wall. In the center, on a low table, three champagne flutes and petits fours were waiting on a silver tray.

— You're right in for the aperitif, said Annie.

Philippe then led Adrien into the dining room where a table with three place settings was set. Two silver candlesticks with candles decorated the table. Philippe later showed a large bedroom with a large double bed with an iron frame and two bedside tables stuffed with books.

— This is our bed, but we will leave it to you during your stay with us. You will be more comfortable there. Annie has made room for you in the cupboard to put your things down, said Philippe, pointing to the large lacquered wood cupboard.

For the moment, Adrien was content to put his bag at the foot of the bed to continue the visit more at ease.

An office adjoined the bedroom. Two separate computers sat on it, and shelves filled with books, knick-knacks and boxes adorned the room. Next door, in a guest bedroom, two single beds had been prepared. Annie and Philippe had decided to sleep there for the comfort of their visitor.

Nearby was the marble bathroom with a shower stall with many jets. A little further on, a small functional kitchen was used to prepare meals.

— Welcome home, young man, said Philippe. Hope you have a good time there.

Adrien nodded. He hoped so too. The two sixties were likeable, but he wondered what had taken him to embark on this escapade.

They returned to the living room where Adrien took a seat on a sofa and Annie and Philippe on the other. Philippe uncorked a bottle of champagne and filled the flutes. Annie had prepared toast of foie gras and fish terrine. They toasted and attacked the appetizers.

— What can we do for you during your stay here? Philippe asked after having exchanged a few small talk about the weather.

Adrien understood that he was talking about the sexual part of the stay. On their announcement, the two retirees had indicated that they were open to all proposals.

— I don't know, it's the first time I've booked a Sex and Bed.

Annie and Philippe looked at each other and laughed before admitting that they too were offering this type of accommodation for the first time.

— Our ad had been online for a few minutes when your registration reached us, said Annie. We were happy, we didn't think it would go so quickly.

— I was hesitating when your ad appeared on the site. The photos of your apartment decided me. Why did you register on this site?

An embarrassed silence settled between Annie and Philippe who threw Annie a reproachful look before explaining himself.

— Annie has serious gambling problems both online and at the casino. She lost a lot of our savings. We already had to sell her jewelry. The ones she wears are just junk. We need money to maintain our lifestyle and stay in our apartment.

— I lost a lot and I promised not to play Philippe again if we got out of this bad patch. I got banned from all casinos and no longer have access to our bank accounts or a credit card. I will do my best to make your stay as pleasant as possible in order to obtain a good evaluation from you and quickly get us back on track.

— Your satisfaction is very important to us in order to quickly obtain other customers, said Philippe.

Adrien finished his flute of champagne. He understood the motivations of his unusual hosts a little better.

— Do you want me to suck you? Annie asked. It's my fault that we're here, I have to make an effort to be forgiven for Philippe.

Adrien looked at Annie's mouth: it was large with full lips. It would probably be nice to put your tail there. Annie was staring at his crotch for a physical reaction from him.

Not to be outdone, Philippe offered to jerk him off.

Adrien didn't know what to do. He was mostly tired from his journey and felt all sweaty.

— Before I would like to shower if you don't mind.

— I put a bathrobe and a towel for you in the bathroom. Make yourselves at home.

Adrien thanked them. He undressed in the bedroom and walked naked to the bathroom. In the shower cubicle, he ran the hot water over him which carried away the perspiration and fatigue of his journey. He soaped himself, insisting on his penis so that it was clean and rinsed himself while considering the choices that were offered to him. Madame had been quicker, so he decided to accept her offer. Monsieur would be patient to offer his services. He was there for three days, he would have time to reserve a moment for him. He put on his bathrobe and returned to the living room where Annie and Philippe were waiting for him.

With a determined step, he went to Annie and opened his bathrobe a little, revealing his penis, indicating that he accepted her proposal. Annie looked at Adrien's cock in front of her eyes. The sex was long and began to swell. He appeared vigorous and a well-groomed brown fleece surrounded him. After a moment's hesitation, Annie grabbed Adrien's cock and brought it to her mouth. Very quickly, Adrien's cock swelled and lengthened. Annie held the penis with one hand and sucked the end with pleasure.

— How long it is, she said. I'll never be able to put it whole in my mouth. Longer than yours my Philippe.

She felt Adrien's cock to check its strength and noted that it was also harder than that of her husband.

— So suck this young man instead of comparing his cock to mine, Philippe got on his nerves. It is because of you that we are here. So, assume and put your heart into it.

Annie resumed sucking Adrien energetically under the watchful eye of her husband. She wasn't as good as Tony, but she was trying hard. It didn't take long for drool to flow from the corners of her lips, staining her black dress. Beside her, Philippe lost nothing of the show. Watching his wife suck another cock turned him on and it wasn't long before he stroked her cock through the fabric of his pants.

— Get your cock out, you'll stain your suit and you'll have to take it to the dyer. You know we don't have the means at the moment, said Annie who saw him out of the corner of her eye.

Crestfallen, Philippe did so and began to caress himself. His cock was still soft, but it wasn't long before she firmed up. With amusement, Adrien had witnessed the scene. Annie was now licking his cock greedily making little sucking noises. Out of clumsiness, she sometimes also bit her teeth, but Adrien appreciated her ardor.

So as not to tire her too much, Adrien did not try to restrain himself and quickly discharged himself into her mouth. With a groan, he sent her mash before removing his cock from Annie's mouth. A large drop of semen fell on Annie's dress, above her breast, forming a large stain.

Annie closed her mouth and swallowed suddenly to avoid tasting the precious liquid.

— Um, that was hot. It had been a long time since I had tasted this.

Next to them, Philippe, his cock outstretched, was in despair that it was already over. Seeing his confusion, Annie offered to finish it.

— Otherwise he might be grumpy all evening, she said, moving towards him.

She knelt on top of his cock and began to pump him in turn to make him come.

Adrien sat down and watched the couple do their business as he wiped his penis in the bathrobe provided. He enjoyed this stay more and more.

Philippe ends up groaning with pleasure by letting go in the mouth of his tender lover who carefully collected his cum before swallowing it too.

— I'm not going to be hungry anymore with everything you put in my mouth, gentlemen, she said, wiping her lips with a small napkin.

She then went to the kitchen to prepare the meal while Adrien and Philippe finished their aperitif. Philippe closed his pants and poured champagne again. The discussion began without shame between the two men who had come to enjoy in the mouth of the same woman. Philippe was a retired aeronautical engineer. He had made a very good living, but his wife was a gamer and spent more than he earned.

— She has many faults, but I love her and I cannot do without her.

— Is she the one who wanted to register for Sex and Bed?

— Yes. I wonder if she hadn't planned her move to spice up our sex life which was dead calm.

— Do you plan to receive other travelers?

— A certain number, the time to remake us. We would even like to earn a little more to give ourselves a nice cruise, but I don't know if that will work. We haven't had any other registrations yet. Hardly a few requests for information to find out how far we were from the sea.

Annie then called them to sit down to eat. Adrien remained in a bathrobe. Annie had prepared salad and lasagna and Philippe uncorked a bottle of red wine.

The discussion began around Adrien's wishes during his stay.

— I plan to walk on the Croisette and see the Palais des Festivals. Climb the stairs. Maybe, bathe if the weather allows it.

— You can swim all year round here if you are brave.

Philippe spoke to Adrien about the Lerins islands which were to be visited as well as the Suquet hill which was the cradle of Cannes. Adrien had not yet stopped his program. He would see tomorrow.

For dessert, Annie served a chocolate pear. Philippe offered a digestif, but Adrien was not keen on strong alcohol. They chatted for a while and then decided to go to bed.

Annie and Philippe brushed their teeth then put on their pajamas. Adrien had only to take off his bathrobe. He was sleeping naked. Annie wore trousers and a button-down shirt with small multicolored patterns while Philippe had donned a gray cotton nightgown that ended above the knees. Adrien told himself that in bed it was Madame who wore the pants and not Monsieur.

— Do you want one of us to sleep with you? Annie asked.

The question surprised Adrien who answered without thinking that he wanted Monsieur to come with him. Philippe was sympathetic to him and his outfit amused him.

A little disappointed, Annie wished them a good night between boys and went to her room.

Adrien and Philippe stretched out on the large bed under the duvet. The mattress was comfortable and the pillows soft.

— Thank you for choosing me. I like the comfort of my bed, says Philippe.

— Between men, we must support each other. You shouldn't give up your bed to your next customers.

— That's what I thought.

Philippe took a book from the bedside table and began to read the biography of a retired general. On his cell phone, Adrien checked his Instagram account before looking at what was on the Madame's bedside table. She slept with a night mask and also read books. Adrien picked up a paperback from a philosopher whose name he had heard, but dropped it after barely a paragraph.

Beside him, Philippe was immersed in his reading. Adrien wondered why he had chosen her when he refused to have a homosexual relationship with his friend Tony. Was it the effect of the nightgown? He then wondered if he would appreciate having a homosexual relationship that went beyond a simple fellatio. He slipped his hand under the duvet and saw that Philippe's nightgown was pulled up to the middle of his legs. He ran his hand under it and touched Mister's cock. The cock was soft and the skin on his balls wrinkled. His bush hardly maintained. He then played for a while with Philippe's sex without saying anything. It was pretty fun. He tried to jerk it off, but the man's cock was struggling to get up.

— Since my prostate operation, the preliminaries are longer, apologized Philippe, putting down his book. Maybe you would like me to suck you like Annie did?

While wiggling Philippe's cock, Adrien was thinking. Maybe it was time to try something else.

— I'd rather fuck you, said the young man.

Philippe jumped. A moment of embarrassment invaded him.

— I never did that, he said.

— Me neither, assured Adrien.

Although Tony begged him to put it on him, Adrien had never wanted to go all the way with him so as not to mar their beautiful friendship.

Philippe remained thoughtful. Adrien did not know if the sixty-year-old would accede to his request, however the cock between his fingers had stiffened.

All right, said Philippe. I'm willing to try if it doesn't hurt.

— I'll be careful, Adrien promised. I have lube in my bag and I'll go smoothly.

Adrien took the tube from his bag and asked Philippe to get on all fours on the bed. He pulled her nightgown up to her stomach and let some lubricant flow between Philippe's buttocks before starting to massage her anus to dilate it and insert the tip of a finger.

— Oh ! said Philippe.

— It's nothing, it's just my finger. Is it unpleasant?

— No, it's surprising, but it's better than a colonoscopy.

Tacitly, Adrien continued to massage her asshole before pushing his finger deeper, making Philippe cries out as his cock hardened. Adrien fondly stroked his tail, making the sixty-year-old purr with pleasure before going any further. After putting a finger in Philippe, Adrien decided to spend two to prepare him to welcome his tail.

— Oh ! What are you doing boy

— I'll put the tips of two fingers up your ass. It hurts you ?

— No, no continue.

Adrien began to move back and forth with his fingers in Philippe's anus. The old man groaned with pleasure. His penis drooled over the bed. For a moment, Adrien hesitated to put three fingers up her ass, but that would have been too much for the moment. Philippe now had a powerful erection. His hard cock stood proudly under her belly. Philippe appreciated the experience.

Adrien then pushed his two fingers deeper, triggering cries of pleasure.

— Oh yes ! Oh yes ! Its good !

Attracted by the noise, Annie stuck her head to the bedroom door. She was then surprised to see her husband on all fours, his shirt up, being fucked in the ass.

— Oh yes ! Oh yes! How good it is, Philippe chuckled.

Annie motioned for Adrien to be silent. She did not want to disturb her husband during his pleasure.

Adrien took Annie's night mask from the bedside table and passed it to Philippe to hide his eyes.

— You will feel better the sensations in your ass as well, he justified.

— Thank you, but continue it's too good.

— I'll relax your anus a little bit after I'll put my cock in your ass.

— Give it to me gently above all.

Adrien put the gel back on his fingers and continued to work Philippe's asshole. The anus was now well dilated and Adrien could slide his fingers better and better in the passage.

Annie took advantage that her husband did not see her to enter the bedroom and sat down with her back against the cupboard in front of the bed so as not to lose any of the spectacle. She slipped her hand into the bottom of her pajamas and began to stroke herself as she watched her husband get his ass fucked hard.

Judging the time had come to go further, Adrien put down his lubricant and stood behind Philippe. He grabbed his cock and placed it in front of Philippe's orifice and leaned against it.

— I'll put it on you, he warned.

— I smell something. It's bigger and hotter.

Adrien pressed his cock against the anus and inserted his penis in Philippe's buttocks.

— Where there! What is that ?

— My cock, I'm going to enter it gently so as not to hurt you, but it's tight.

— Don't stop my boy, said Philippe excitedly.

In front of the cupboard, Annie was in all her forms. His face was sweating. She rubbed her pussy vigorously, biting her lips so as not to moan and betray his presence.

Carefully Adrien pushed his machine into Philippe, advancing slowly in him to spare him.

— Where it is good! Oh that's good ! Are you all there my boy?

— No, barely a third.

— A third. I feel like you're going to split my stomach in half. That you're shoving an iron bar through my stomach!

— You want me to stop ?

— Not at all. I have never been so excited. Keep on going. Do yourself a favor, said Philippe, stretching out his hand to pull himself on the penis.

With his last strength, Philippe masturbated vigorously.

Adrien continued to sink into Philippe. He walked slowly and cautiously, making small round trips in Philippe's anus, pushing each time a little further into the old man's ass.

Philippe's anus was tighter than a vagina, but Adrien's cock was there, tight and warm. The feeling was different, but the fun was there. Adrien felt he liked it.

— I put it deeper, said Adrien.

— How many ? How many ? asked Philippe.

— Two-thirds.

— There are still some outside!

— A little bit, almost nothing.

— Put me all my boy. Go ahead !

— Are you sure ?

— Yes go ahead ! Please !

Adrien grabbed Philippe by the hips and began to pound him, first coming back and then gradually trying to go further. He was going to give her everything. Philippe demanded it. We had to go to the end. Under these bumps, the old man moaned with pleasure.

Annie was on the verge of ecstasy. The hand in her pajamas was waving frantically and with the other, she was squeezing her small breasts.

Adrien made several back and forth movements, hesitating to push the last stop, but Philippe demanded to push it to the end.

— I'm going, Adrien warned before pushing hard with his cock and pulling Philippe's buttocks to him.

Suddenly, he entered his entire tail in Philippe, banging his balls against the buttocks of the sexagenarian.

— Ha! cried Philippe as a flood of sperm came out of her sex.

The front of her body collapsed on the mattress and only her buttocks remained up with Adrien's cock in them to carry them.

— How good my boy. I didn't think it was possible to cum so hard.

— I haven't finished, said Adrien.

— Go ahead, do what you have to do, said Philippe defeated.

Adrien activated in the buttocks of the sexagenarian. The old man's asshole was now perfectly relaxed and Adrien could move faster and faster inside him. He was banging hard against his buttocks, each time tearing out cries from Philippe.

— I'm going to cum inside you, said Adrien.

— Go ahead my boy, whispered Philippe.

After a final stop, Adrien dropped his mash in Philippe's asshole. To the depths of what he could stick his cock into her. He hung on her butt for a moment before releasing them with a coarse groan. Slowly, he withdrew from Philippe when a violent cry resounded in the room.

— Haaa! Annie yelled, startling the two men.

Philippe took off the night mask and saw his wife leaning against the cupboard so as not to collapse. She had just enjoyed uttering a powerful cry from the bottom of her guts. She pulled a wet hand out of her pajamas as a large stain formed on her crotch. The pleasure she had seen her Philippe getting fucked in the ass was such that she had soaked her pajamas.

— Sorry, I couldn't help myself. I'm all upset to have seen you get fucked in the ass.

A powerful stream of liquid had poured into her nightgown. Unable to stay that way, Annie undressed and put on clean pajamas. Her skin was wrinkled in places and her pussy graying. Annie no longer knew where she was.

With a kleenex, Philippe wiped his anus where semen was flowing.

Exhausted, Adrien sank down on the bed. He had given everything and wanted to sleep now. Philippe slipped under the duvet. Devastated and upset by what had just happened to him, he was no more than a shadow of himself.

With envy, Annie approached Adrien.

— Tomorrow, can you bugger me too? I want to know what it does. With my Philippe, we never dared to try and, after what I just saw, I really want to go there too.

— Okay, Adrien promised before he too slipped into bed and turned off the light.

Annie went to her room and Philippe fell asleep immediately.

In bed, Adrien smiles: his stay in Cannes started off well.

Adrien's promise

The smell of brioche woke Adrien from his sleep. It took him a few seconds to locate where he was and remember that he had taken a Sex and Bed in Cannes. Philippe was no longer next to him, but he could hear his voice nearby. He stretched and stood up, put on a robe and walked to the dining room.

Around the wooden table, Annie and Philippe were sharing their breakfast. There was fruit, juice, hot brioche and jam.

Adrien sat down with them. After being sucked and buggered Philippe, a certain bond was born between them. Annie served him coffee and Philippe offered him orange juice. Adrien spread himself on the brioche.

— What are your plans for today? Annie asked.

— I want to visit Cannes, I came for that after all.

— It's going to be nice, said Philippe.

Through the window, the sun was already illuminating the city.

— You haven't forgotten your promise? Annie asked.

Adrien took a few seconds to remember that he had promised to fuck Annie.

— No of course, but you want to do this immediately after breakfast?

— No, I have my yoga class. You can take care of my behind after your ride.

— It will be with pleasure, committed Adrien.

— Perfect, said Annie before getting up and going to get ready for her gym class.

The two men remained around the table. Adrien had a good appetite. The two sixties had shown him that they still had some under the hood despite their age.

— What Annie saw yesterday turned her all over. As soon as I got up, she asked me about how I felt. I had to tell him everything in great detail. Your stay with us calls into question many of our certainties.

Dressed in tight purple sweatpants, Annie greeted them and set off for her yoga class. She needed it for her aching joints.

— I'm going to go get myself ready, Adrien said after finishing his coffee.

— Will you eat with us this afternoon? asked Philippe.

— I do not know.

Adrien got up and went to the room where he got naked. As he searched his backpack for new clothes, he noticed Philippe's presence at the entrance to the bedroom. The old man looked upset.

— I'd like to ask you a favor.

— What can I do for you ? If it's putting a glowing review on Sex and Bed, that's okay. I have had an incredible stay with you.

— No, that's not it. Yesterday, you made me discover new horizons and I too would like to taste your sperm, like Annie. Can I jerk you off?

In surprise, Adrien froze. He hadn't expected such a proposal, but he didn't want to refuse. Philippe seemed to want it. Still naked as a worm, Adrien stretched out on the bed and Philippe came to stand next to him. Philippe was still wearing his gray cotton nightgown. With his wrinkled hand, he began to fiddle with Adrien's cock with emotion. Very quickly, Adrien's tail swelled. Philippe then began to move back and forth above, but his gestures were awkward. He didn't have Tony's address.

— It's new to me, he said. Am I doing well?

— Yes it's not bad. You can hold it more firmly, you won't break it.

— Can I lick it for you?

— If you want.

Philippe leaned over and began to suck his cock. His first licks were hesitant, but soon he improved. Adrien was starting to take a liking to it and he pushed his cock a little more into Philippe's mouth. With his goatee, Philippe stroked his balls, the feeling was pleasant.

Adrien was not long in being excited. He reached out to Philippe's cock and began to jerk it off. Vigorously, he tugged at her, and it wasn't long before the old man chuckled with pleasure. His cock quickly became hard and Adrien decided to milk him like a cow.

— Oh that's good boy.

— I will not be long in coming, warns Adrien.

— Tell me I'm keeping it in my mouth.

Adrien was sucked for a little while longer then he asked Philippe not to move. His cock was the mouth of the sexagenarian when Adrien was crossed by a groan and released his mash.

At the same time, Philippe ejaculated in Adrien's hand.

Greedily, Philippe collected all of Adrien's sperm in his mouth. He kept it for a moment to assess the taste, then swallowed it.

— Thank you Adrien, I wanted to have done that at least once in my life after being fucked in the ass.

— You're welcome, said Adrien before jumping out of bed and going quickly to take a shower.

He then put on shorts and a t-shirt and left the apartment, leaving Philippe all exhilarated by his new experiences.

•

Adrien set off on foot towards the seaside. In barely twenty minutes, he reached the Croisette and headed for the Palais des Festivals. The red carpet walked by the biggest stars was still in place. Adrien couldn't resist the pleasure of climbing the steps and taking a selfie in front of the building which he posted on Instagram.

Adrien continued his walk to the port where a shuttle would soon leave for the Lerins Islands. Adrien bought his ticket and sat in the back of the boat.

These vacations did him good. He had hardly left his house since his aunt's death when there were many beautiful places to discover.

I have to do something with my life Adrien said to himself.

The shuttle left for the islands with few passengers on board. Adrien felt good on the water. He felt like he was living a unique moment. He went down to the first island in order to discover the paths and the small coves. In a snack bar near the pier, he bought a sandwich and drinks and set off on an adventure. Other walkers imitated him, but very quickly Adrien found himself alone on the pedestrian paths of the island. He walked under the pines to a small secluded cove where he decided to stop. On the island, he felt like he was in paradise.

After bathing, Adrien lay down on his towel where he ended up falling asleep.

He spent the day in the cove and only left to catch the last shuttle.

On the return trip, Adrien then remembered his promise to Annie.

I must keep my word he says to him.

•

After doing a search on his cell phone, Adrien made a detour to a shop located in a parallel to the station. Inside, the seller offered him a gift package for his purchase, but Adrien didn't need it.

Adrien then joined Annie and Philippe's apartment. Philippe had abandoned his suit for beige pants and a casual shirt. Anne wore a long black pleated skirt with a white blouse parted up to the level of her small breasts. She seemed to be impatiently awaiting Adrien's return.

Adrien took a quick shower to get the salt out of his skin and then found Annie and Philippe in the living room for an aperitif. Philippe had served himself a single malt with an ice cube. Annie was sipping a suze and Adrien took a glass of Bandol rosé.

Out of politeness, Philippe asked him how his day had gone. Adrien told them about his visit to Cannes and the Lerins Islands. Annie said nothing and listened to them. When Adrien had finished, she returned to the charge concerning her case.

— Will you finally be able to take care of my ass?

— Yes, said Adrien. I also have a surprise for you.

— Ha good? Annie rejoices.

Adrien went to get a small bag and took out a black and oval object a little more tapering on one side and the other with a rod and a shine. He took it out and showed it to Annie who asked him what it was.

— An anal plug. Since you've never been taken this route before, it would be nice to prepare the ground by placing this object in your butt so that your anus will get used to having something inside. This will save you pain.

— How attentive Adrien is. What should I do ?

— Get on all fours on the sofa and pull up your skirt, I will install this plug in your buttocks with lubricant before you assfuck.

— Finally some good news, rejoices Annie.

Enthusiastically, she settled into the requested position and lifted her skirt revealing two big white flabby buttocks with a black thong in the middle.

With a delicate gesture, Adrien moved the string and using the lubricant, he began to massage Annie's anus. Philippe observed the scene without missing a beat.

— Do you like Annie? he asked.

— It's surprising and pleasant. I never thought I'd use my butt to do this.

— Put a finger in his ass, boy, that will do him good, said Philippe.

Adrien questioned Annie with a glance, but the latter was delighted. Gently, Adrien put a phalanx in Annie's asshole.

— Oh ! What is that ?

— A tip of my finger. Can i continue?

— Go ahead my little Adrien.

Adrien continued to work it carefully while pushing his finger into Annie's buttocks. The sixty-year-old moaned with pleasure. Adrien then took the plug and presented it at the entrance to Annie's anus. He pushed and introduced it inside the buttocks of the sixty-year-old who chuckled with pleasure. Only the shine was now visible between the buttocks, the oval shape was all inside Annie's ass.

— The plug will relax the anus so that penetration is then more pleasant for you.

— How do you feel? asked Philippe.

— It's strange to have something in the buttocks, but it's good.

Annie pulled down her skirt and stood up. Her body was evaluating what she had in the buttocks. She took a few steps and smiled.

— Thanks Adrien. It's weird, but it doesn't bother me.

Annie then left to take care of the meal by wiggling her buttocks. She seemed to enjoy walking around with a plug in her ass.

Philippe watched her walk away, delighted that his wife appreciated.

— I'm glad she tried the experiment when she has always been cautious on that side.

— Looks like she can't wait for me to fuck her.

— She's only thought about that all day.

— And you, didn't your ass hurt too much last night?

— It's nothing compared to the foot I took. Where did you find this plug?

— In a sex shop next to the station.

— Are there other models?

— Full, including much larger plugs, more than twenty-five centimeters for the most imposing, handcuffs, sexy outfits ...

— I'll have to go take a look, said Philippe, stroking his goatee.

Adrien and Philippe talked for a while about sex shops and sex toys, although Adrien often just repeated what Tony had told him. Annie then invited them to sit down to eat. She had prepared a roast beef with potatoes and was smiling broadly, constantly waddling her buttocks. Philippe opened a bottle of Bordeaux to accompany the meat.

Annie sat down delicately on his bottom. She seemed to enjoy having an object in her ass.

— How do you feel ? asked Philippe.

— Very good, but I can't wait to move on. I'm wet my thong. It had been a long time since I had been turned on like this.

Adrien smiled: Annie's pleasure was genuine and he now wanted to fuck her too, even if he had never thought of fucking an old woman before coming here.

Although succulent, the dish was shipped like the chocolate mousse prepared by Philippe. Without lingering, they decided to go to bed. Philippe retrieved his nightgown in the bedroom and asked to attend Annie's sodomy.

— No way, protested the latter. I want to enjoy it alone.

— But my dear, you saw me get fucked in the ass.

— This has nothing to do with. I want to be alone with Adrien. You just have to go jerk off in front of a porn video on your computer if you want to cum.

Reluctantly, Philippe gave in and left them. Annie carefully closed the bedroom door and asked Adrien what to do.

— Make yourself comfortable and undress, Adrien said, doing the same.

— Getting my ass fucked for the first time at my age, I'm already all upset, said Annie.

She lifted her skirt and blouse. She was not wearing a bra and found herself in a black thong with a plug in her ass. Her skin was loose in places and she was overweight on her stomach and buttocks. With a sensual gesture, she slid her black thong to the ground revealing a gray fleece provided, but well maintained. The borders had been made a short time ago.

— He's always well dressed, Annie asked, turning and showing her ass to Adrien.

— Yes, but it's time to get him up and take you from behind.

— With pleasure.

Annie got down on all fours on the bed and wiggled her buttocks. Adrien approached her and played with the plug, having fun lifting it up and putting it back on.

— Do you want me to lubricate your anus a little more and that I first introduce one or two fingers?

— No, put your long, hard cock in it. I have already waited all day.

Annie then turned to Adrien and touched his cock to make sure of the hardness of Adrien's cock and could not resist the urge to give him a few languid licks.

— Take me quickly, she begged.

Adrien positioned himself behind her and moved his cock near Annie's anus.

— I will put it.

— Go ahead !

With ease, Adrien thrust his penis in Annie's ass and then put half of his cock between her buttocks.

— Oh ! Oh that's good ! cried Annie.

— You don't hurt?

— No, continue.

Adrien began to move back and forth in Annie's ass who began to moan with pleasure and cry.

— Oh yes ! Its good. Smash me.

The old woman was very excited.

Encouraged by these cries, Adrien accelerated his movements and decided to push his cock a little further into Annie's ass, who reacted by screaming more and more loudly with pleasure.

— Put me whole there.

— It might hurt.

— I don't care, I want to.

Adrien took a swing from the pelvis and entered his entire cock into Annie's ass who cried out with pleasure.

— Haaa!

— Do you feel it?

— Oh yeah, you're ripping my ass.

Adrien wriggled into Annie's ass making her moan with pleasure. He continued until Annie came with a scream that echoed throughout the apartment. At the same time as she cried, a flood of liquid gushed out of her pussy.

— Oh my little Adrien, it's good, said Annie, collapsing her head on the bed.

— Me too, I will enjoy.

— Go ahead, my ass is yours.

Adrien activated and a few moments later, he released all his cum in Annie's ass. He then withdrew his cock and let himself fall next to Annie sweating: the sexagenarian had exhausted her.

— Thank you for letting me know these feelings, my little Adrien, said Annie.

— You're welcome, it was a pleasure.

Without bothering to put on her pajamas, Annie slipped under the duvet and fell asleep. Adrien was not long in joining her in Morphée's arms.

•

At the start of the morning, Adrien, Annie and Philippe met in the dining room to share their breakfast. Adrien and Philippe seemed more united than ever. Sitting side by side, they were smiling at each other and giving each other languid glances. Adrien didn't know if it was because he had fucked them both or if it was because of these new experiences in which the retirees had launched themselves.

— What do you want to do this morning Adrien? Annie asked, buttering her toast.

— I do not know. I have my train in the early afternoon. I must return to Paris this evening.

— If we can still give you a good time, do not hesitate, said Philippe.

Adrien thinks about what he would like. He had been sucked and fucked Annie and Philippe, but he hadn't even lowered Annie from the front. He would have liked to put his young cock in her old pussy to see the effect it was having.

— I would like to take Annie before leaving.

Philippe looked at his wife to know his opinion.

— With pleasure, I want to too, said Annie. But let's not delay, I don't want to make you miss your train.

— Can I watch this time? asked Philippe.

— Of course my love, said Annie kissing her.

Annie dipped her toast in her coffee and ate it. They then cleared the table and went to the bedroom.

— I wouldn't have kept my pajamas on for long, said Annie undressing.

Adrien only had to take off his bathrobe while Philippe sat down on a chair and pulled up his nightgown to stroke his penis.

When Adrien lay down on Annie, he already had a hard cock. He felt Annie's aged but warm flesh against his skin and carefully inserted his cock inside her pussy. Annie's pussy was already wet. Adrien's cock entered it all by itself, like a lump of melted butter, and he began to work it in the missionary position.

It wasn't long before Annie moaned with pleasure and asked for more.

— Come on boy, stuff me.

Adrien was banging her in the pussy, avoiding going too hard so as not to hurt her. Annie moaned with pleasure under the loving gaze of Philippe whose sex was erect.

— Come join me, my Philippe, called Annie suddenly. Come put it in my mouth.

Without being asked, Philippe approached and began to get sucked while Adrien continued to kick Annie's pussy.

29

Annie was in heaven. She had a hard and vigorous cock inside her and took care of her husband's cock with her mouth. It wasn't long before she came, releasing a flood of liquid on Adrien.

After a few more strokes of the cock, Adrien cums inside Annie until the last drop before pulling back and dropping to the side.

— Come and enjoy me too, Annie asked Philippe.

Her husband lay down on her in turn and pounded her until he too emptied himself into her pussy. When he pulled back, a trickle of cum was dripping from Annie's graying pussy.

Resting on the bed, Adrien and Philippe surrounded Annie. Everyone had a smile.

— What was good, said Annie.

— It will have been a great stay, said Adrien.

•

After a long train journey punctuated by delays, Adrien returned to Paris. By metro, he reached the 14th arrondissement and walked to his apartment building. In his mailbox, several advertisements had been placed as well as a letter from his aunt's lawyer.

He went up to his apartment and opened the envelope. Inside, the lawyer had written him a letter.

"Dear Mr. Adrien Leguen,

In accordance with your aunt's last wishes, I invite you three months after her death to find me in my study in order to specify the testamentary conditions that will allow you to benefit from her fortune.

In the event that you neglect this meeting, its assets will be frozen before being transmitted to an environmental protection association.

While waiting to receive you in my study, please accept, Mr. Adrien Leguen, my respectful greetings.

Your devoted lawyer.

Adrien read the letter several times. When they first met, the notary had not spoken to him at all about testamentary conditions.

Damn, what has that old goat got planned, cursed Adrien.

Viviane's last wishes

A little tense, Adrien went to see Edmond Delacroix, his aunt's lawyer. His study was in a mansion on the hill of Montmartre. Edmond was close to Viviane. Adrien had seen him many times at her house during receptions.

Several employees worked in the study in muffled silence. The atmosphere was marked by solemnity and discretion.

While he waited in a waiting room with many magazines on a low table, Adrien wondered what his aunt had in store for him. He did not expect to return to the notary after reading the will designating him as sole heir just three months ago.

Adrien did not wait long before Edmond Delacroix received him in his large office, probably larger than his two-room apartment. The man in his fifties was tall and fat. He wore a light gray suit and a white shirt stretched out by his overweight. His handshake was limp and his cheeks plump.

— How are you Adrien? he asked after inviting her to sit down.

— It's okay, said the young man who had never liked his aunt too much.

Edmond picked up a heavy file from his desk from which he took a letter folded in half.

— Your aunt left us before she had time to introduce you to her business. She was planning on showing you what she was doing starting in your twenty-fifth year.

Adrien was unaware of his aunt's intentions. They spoke little to each other and their exchanges were rather platonic. He knew that she was rich and that she had built her fortune on her own, but he didn't really know what her business was. She had always been discreet about her activities.

The lawyer cleared his throat and began to read the mail in his hands.

My little Adrien,

If Edmond is reading this letter to you, it is because something has happened to me sooner than expected. I haven't always been so caring to you that I should have been, but you reminded me too much of my younger brother.

I want the best for you, that's why I'm going to help you beyond death. It is important that you get to know me better and that you understand what I have achieved and undertaken. Here are my last wishes to accompany you in your life.

First of all, you're going to come back to my apartment, at least for a year.

You will also have to obtain a higher education diploma. The one you want, but a diploma.

Then I want you to check out my stuff. Ludivine, my assistant, will help you. Edmond has extended his contract.

Finally, you have to get out of your bubble a little and discover the world. For this, you will make five trips to places where I have been.

Edmond will check that you respect these last wishes before handing you full ownership of all my fortune, which is estimated at over 120 million euros.

Life is difficult Adrien, but it deserves to be lived.

Your aunt who loved you.

Viviane

At the end of his reading, the lawyer crushed a tear in his eye with his coiled finger. Viviane's last wishes had moved him.

— I miss her so much, he sniffed. She was a true friend.

— I didn't really know her.

— She wanted to spend more time with you. Did you understand these last wishes?

— Yes, I'm going to go home, said Adrien, who didn't really want to.

He appreciated his little two-room apartment where he had acquired his independence.

— Go home now, said the lawyer.

— What about the other conditions?

— I'll be there to guide you. Come see me whenever you want and I'll explain these things to you. I have at my disposal a list of all his property and assets. It will help you see clearly.

Edmond walked Adrien to the door of his office and in a gesture that Adrien did not expect, he took him in his arms and hugged him, as if he wanted to feel Viviane's presence again.

— Take care of yourself and come back to see me.

Adrien nodded and left him. He walked to the Sacré Coeur and observed the view over Paris. He was going to move and join his aunt's large apartment in the 16th arrondissement. It only remained for him to prepare his things.

The apartment

A large bag on his shoulder and his suitcase in hand, Adrien went to the 16th arrondissement. Her aunt's apartment was on rue la Tasse, opposite the Trocadero gardens.

It was weird for Adrien to come back here. His aunt had greeted him after his parents died in a car accident, but he had never been able to get along with her or communicate. Now Viviane wanted him to know her better when she had spent her time keeping him away from her.

He took out the key to the building and went up to the 4th where his aunt had the whole floor. The apartment had more than sixteen rooms. Adrien entered and found the smells he knew. Fresh flowers were even in the hall. Adrien wondered who had brought them. He closed the door behind him. Nothing had changed. He almost expected to see his aunt come out of a room.

Adrien was tempted to settle in the small room at the back of the apartment where he had lived for several years, but he ended up opting for a room overlooking the gardens of the Trocadero with a small balcony and a bathroom. There were four bedrooms in addition to her aunt's. It was not the place that was lacking.

Walking around the apartment, Adrien noticed a few paintings and knick-knacks that weren't there on his last visit. The largest room was the living-dining room with its long sofas where one could lie down while watching television and where on the other side, a long glass table with twelve wrought iron chairs allowed his aunt to entertain. his friends.

Nearby was her aunt's office. At the start of the play, a small desk with a wheelchair had been added. Open mail was lying on it. The lawyer had told him about an assistant. Adrien remembered a rather strong little blonde that he had seen with his aunt.

The door to a room was locked. Adrien didn't know what was inside. In the apartment there was also a gym, a library and especially her aunt's bedroom. Everything had remained as it was as if she was going to come back when her body had started to rot at Père-Lachaise.

In front of Viviane's large bedroom, Adrien dreaded entering his private space. A large four-poster bed occupied the central space with opposite a chest of drawers with a large mirror. A section of wall had been converted into a dressing room.

Adrien entered the bedroom. The room was still infused with Channel # 5 fragrance.

Why does she want me to know her when she was just avoiding me?

Adrien slid the panels of the dressing room. All his clothes were neatly stored. Dozens of shoes were lined up next to each other. For a moment, Adrien sat down on the bed. How was he going to find out more about her when she was no longer there? Who was she really?

Slender and overflowing with energy, Viviane seemed to want to devour the world. She always had several projects at the same time and had a thousand activities. Adrien approached the chest of drawers and opened the first drawer. Inside, cosmetics, night creams and other treatments were stored. When Adrien opened the second drawer, he was surprised to discover many sex toys arranged next to each other. There were at least thirty of them with lubricant, geisha balls, vibrators and two strap-on dildos. Adrien had never seen so many and never imagined that his aunt indulges in this kind of pleasures. She had never spoken to him about sex and was very discreet about her partners. Adrien had barely seen her two or three times with the same man, and he had never known of a serious relationship. He examined a few sex toys including a black butt plug nearly four inches wide. He found it hard to imagine his aunt being so tiny sticking it all up her ass.

Adrien opened the last drawer and found a pair of handcuffs, two riding crops and plenty of sexy underwear. There were see-through babydolls, panties open on the buttocks and the genitals, fine lace, stockings, scarves and thongs so small and so thin that it was difficult to imagine what they were hiding.

The naughty, she hid her game well, thought Adrien.

Rummaging through her aunt's things excited him. He wanted to know more about this aunt of whom he ignored many aspects of her personality. In his pants, his cock was swollen and examining his underwear only made matters worse. Between his fingers, he gently touched the lace underwear, imagining his aunt with it. He took black panties all in lace which should not hide anything. The panties had an opening at the level of the sex so that Madame can be penetrated without having to lift her panties. Adrien would never have imagined his stern aunt wearing this, but considering the material in the dresser, she must have done more than carry them.

I did not know her, Adrien said to himself.

He now had his cock tight in his pants and as he watched the panties open at the crotch he walked over to the four-poster bed and lay down on it. He pulled down his pants and boxers, took out his gear and began to stroke himself. The mattress was comfortable and soft. Sex in the air, Adrien began to masturbate in his aunt's lace panties. She had asked him to get to know him better and in doing so, he felt like he was getting closer to her. His penis long and thin was stretched and he wanted to make himself come by defeating in the below.

She would have liked that, Adrien thought to himself, thinking of the sex toys in the drawer.

On his cock, he could feel the fine lace below. He wrapped the panties around his erect penis and began to polish, as if to polish them. Very quickly, his cock became hard and Adrien accelerated his movement. Adrien pulled on his tail thinking of his aunt pushing her sex toys into her private parts. The excitement gained him more and more. He stroked his testicles then activated his penis until he groaned.

— Haaa! he cried, ejaculating underneath, wetting it with cum.

With the panties, he wiped his glans, satisfied to have enjoyed on Viviane's intimate lingerie. His aunt had given him pleasure by making him rub his cock with her underwear. He would never have believed such a thing possible when he came here.

What other secrets is she hiding? Adrien wondered lying on the bed with his cock in the air.

Now he wanted to know more about this aunt he didn't know much about. He was thoughtful when he heard a noise. The front door had just opened. Someone was in the apartment. Hurriedly, he put his boxers and pants back on and figured out what to do with the panties he ended up putting back in the drawer. The underside was wet like his sticky hand, but he didn't have time to rinse it off. He closed the drawer and rushed into the apartment entrance.

Ludivine, the assistant

In the hall, Adrien found himself face to face with a rather strong little blonde with bobbed hair, wearing a black skirt, black stockings and a strict suit of the same color. Tapered glasses hardened her face and made her look stern and sticky.

They looked at each other for a moment without saying anything until the little blonde introduced herself.

— Hello, I am Ludivine Saigneur, Viviane's assistant. You must be Adrien. Maitre Delacroix warned me that you would settle here.

— Yes, said Adrien, a little embarrassed, his cock still wet in his pants.

Ludivine held out her hand to her and Adrien, by reflex, grabbed her realizing too late that she was sticky with cum. Ludivine squeezed it firmly without raising anything.

— Maitre Delacroix asked me to explain your aunt's business to you and to accompany you until the end of my contract.

— That's what he told me.

— I'll tell you everything I know. I am there still eight months, but I will start looking for another job. I cannot afford to be unemployed, especially now that I am getting married.

— Congratulations.

Ludivine showed her a thin ring on her ring finger with a tiny chip of diamond encrusted on it. She got engaged a few months ago and began to prepare for her wedding.

— Viviane often spoke of you. She had a lot of admiration for the only member of her family she had left.

— Well, Adrien wondered.

— Yes, she liked looking at the picture frames on her desk.

Adrien looked at the two frames above. On one, he posed with his parents when he was a child, on the other, he had a glass of champagne in his hand and celebrated the success of his baccalaureate with honors. Viviane had been very proud of him on this occasion.

Ludivine clarified that she put fresh flowers in the hall twice a week. Her aunt loved it. She had continued to do it in remembrance of her.

— Can I stop if you want?

— No, said Adrien, who didn't know his aunt's habit.

— Do you want us to stay in the hall to discuss or can we go to the office? asked Ludivine, who still had her big black bag on her shoulder and her raincoat.

Adrien chooses the office. Ludivine opened a cupboard in the hall and hung up her jacket. Adrien noticed that she had probably known the place better than him since he had left.

— Your aunt would always ask me to make her coffee when I arrived. Do you want one? asked Ludivine.

— Okay, said Adrien, who took the opportunity to go to the bathroom to rinse his hands.

What an idiot, I had my hand full of cum. I hope she hasn't noticed a thing Adrien said to himself.

A few moments later, he joined Ludivine in the office. The small table with the wheelchair at the entrance to the room was his territory. She had put her bag down next to the chair. Behind, on a small piece of furniture, a photocopier was placed.

Ludivine then opened a cabinet in the center of the room revealing a Riviera and Bar coffee machine which crushed the coffee beans before pouring it. Ludivine heated water to infuse a tea bag. She had her back to him to brew the coffee.

Adrien noticed that her buttocks seemed a little tight in her black skirt. The fabric tensed a little too much as she bent down. She was not very pretty: a little too small and a little too strong to be beautiful. Her aunt hadn't recruited her for her looks. She was the most commonplace.

Once the coffee was in the cup, Ludivine handed it to Adrien before returning to his desk, with his mug of tea in hand.

— What do you want to know ? she asked.

— All. I don't know much about my aunt's business. What were you doing for her?

Ludivine gave him a long list of tasks. She answered the phone, opened the mail, sorted her emails, took care of the laundry, reservations ...

— How long have you been working here ?

— Two and a half years. I was having trouble finding a job and your aunt gave me my chance. She taught me a lot.

Ludivine had respect for Viviane, even admiration. Through these words, Adrien discovered a part of his aunt's life that he did not know.

— What's his business?

— She has several buildings, apartments and car parks that she rents in and around Paris through a real estate company. She entrusted the rental to a management company with whom I am often in contact for work agreements, the collection of rents and the collection of unpaid debts. There are also several pending work requests. It also has three restaurants, a tea room and two beauty salons. I go to one of them for waxing and for my nails. The manager gives me a price.

Ludivine listed several other activities for him, including parts in a theater of the golden drop. The assistant had access to a large part of her belongings. Over the years, Viviane had placed her trust in him.

— She also has properties abroad, but Maitre Delacroix knows more about it than I do.

— And his friends ? Do you know any?

— A certain number.

— Did she have someone in her life? There were many men at his funeral.

Embarrassed, Ludivine indicated that she did not take care of Vivianne's private life except to reserve her seats for shows or a table in the restaurant.

— She had a lot of friends and liked to entertain. I often ordered from a local caterer or she had a chef come to my home.

Ludivine had many anecdotes about Viviane. They chatted much of the morning until the young woman noticed the time.

— Oops! I have to go. Usually, I finish later, but I have an appointment for my wedding dress. You have to do it several months in advance to order your dress. My best friend has to join me for the fittings.

— When will the wedding take place?

— Just before the end of my contract. That's why I started looking for another job. Besides, I want to start a family as soon as we get married. I am already thirty-four, I must not delay, said Ludivine before getting up.

Adrien walked her to the door.

Once alone, he reflected on what he had learned. Viviane had many activities and a much fuller life than he had imagined and there were many facets of her personality that he did not know. Fulfilling his last wishes might be more difficult than he had hoped, but now he wanted to get to know better this woman who had taken him in after his parents died.

Movie night

In the evening, Tony joined Adrien at the apartment. It was his day off at the pizzeria. They had decided to have a movie night in front of the big screen in the living room, eating Asian dishes they had ordered. On the coffee table in front of the sofa, in cardboard wrappers, noodles, spring rolls and Asian beers were arranged. Tony hadn't wanted a pizza: he hadn't stopped serving it for ten days.

— Thank you for the invitation, said Tony, to whom Adrien had offered to sleep here.

— You're welcome, with the number of rooms here. There is no lack of space.

Tony had moved into Adrien's old bedroom at the back of the apartment. To be more comfortable for the evening, he had showered when he arrived and changed into a casual outfit: black shorts and a white t-shirt. Adrien was also made more comfortable with jogging and a black t-shirt.

In the dark living room, everyone sat down on a sofa to watch a movie of zombies while eating. The fact that the zombies try to devour men did not stop their appetite. In the end, the heroes smashed the skulls of a horde of zombies launched at their heels.

— Nice Zombiland, said Tony.

— There's nothing better than a monster movie to relax.

Adrien then offered Tony an ice cream. There were bins in the freezer. In the kitchen, they each poured themselves a bowl of chocolate and vanilla ice cream.

— Your aunt's apartment is very nice, said Tony, who had never been there.

— I have to live there for a year, said Adrien, who had confided Viviane's last wishes to Tony.

— At least now you can invite me.

When Adrien lived here, his aunt had never wanted him to bring friends. None of his classmates had ever walked through the front door.

— What are we looking at now? Tony asked.

— What you want, you choose this time, said Adrien.

— There is a new vampire movie on Netflix.

Adrien nodded. At least with Tony, there was no argument over the choice of TV program. They had the same tastes and Tony loved to watch football to tame players in shorts. It wasn't like his last girlfriend who always annoyed him about the choice of film and watched sentimental silliness every night.

Besides, it was still impossible to fuck until the end of the movie, which annoyed Adrien. Maybe that was why their relationship hadn't held up.

In the living room, Tony rushed to the remote. He loved the huge screen that hung on the wall and hooked up to a home theater. While eating their ice cream, they watched a vampire movie where hemoglobin was squirting all the time. Adrien found a pear liqueur to finish the meal. A little drunk, they were good on the sofas.

When the movie ended at over 1 am, they hesitated to start another one. In front of them, on the coffee table, the remains of their meal were spread out. Adrien would tidy up before Ludivine arrived tomorrow morning. He had already shaken her hand full of cum, he didn't want her to think he was living like a pig.

— Do you know what's in the closed room? asked Tony who had visited the apartment.

— No, Ludivine doesn't have the key and I haven't found it.

— You want us to force the door?

— No, I don't want to break it. I'll find that key eventually.

— How is the girl who works here?

— Rather banal, small, a little thick. A strict, even frigid look, but she's due to get married soon. What about you at the pizzeria?

— It's okay, but I have a favor for you. The two bosses are gay and one of them is very jealous. He thinks I want to steal his boyfriend when I told him that I was already in a relationship with someone and that it was serious. He didn't want to believe me and made a scene. You should go to the pizzeria.

— Why ?

— I told them I was with you. I showed your photo to the two bosses.

— Why me ?

— You're the only one I can ask that to. Can you come over and act like you're my boyfriend? Please, otherwise the jealous other won't let go and I might lose my job. I feel good in this pizzeria.

— And the other boss, you dredge him?

— Not at all since I am in a relationship with you and very much in love. Besides, it's a very pale red and I don't like reds.

Tony watched, insisting Adrien who finally agreed. For once Tony was trying to keep his job.

— Ok, I'll come by, Adrien promised.

— When?

— Soon.

— Great, you're a brother.

Tony took his cell phone and stuck to Adrien to take a selfie which he posted on Instagram adding little hearts.

— What are you doing ? asked Adrien.

— I make believe that one is in couple so that the other leaves me. Finally, it would be easier if you accepted to be really my boyfriend. I could give you flowers and give you little gifts.

Adrien grumbled, shrugging his shoulders.

— You're already my best friend, isn't that enough for you?

— Yes, but that's not why I won't like it a little more, Tony said, making her eyes soft.

Adrien loved Tony a lot, but he didn't want to spoil their beautiful friendship and especially break Tony's heart if they broke up or quarreled. Tony was a real artichoke heart.

— Not at the moment, Adrien declined.

— Damn ! Tony groaned, tapping on the couch.

Adrien yawned: he wanted to go to bed now, but Tony was in no rush. His friend had always been a night owl.

— If we can't be together for real, at least I can give you a friend's blowjob, Tony offered.

At this idea, Adrien's cock rose by itself. Tony knew how to suck.

— Don't tell me that the old woman from Cannes pumped you better than me? Tony asked.

— I thought she was going to bite my sausage.

— Cut down on your jogging, Tony said, moving closer to Adrien.

— So I too will make you come to return the favor.

With joy Tony threw his arms up to the sky. With a gesture, he slid his shorts off and took off his t-shirt. He was naked under his shorts and his cock was already standing. Tony didn't have a single hair on his skin or penis. His abs were protruding and his muscles well defined.

Adrien slid his jogging pants and boxers on his feet before removing them. His long cock had already started to quiver.

On the couch, Tony lay down facing Adrien. Tony's head was level with Adrien's cock while the latter could grab his friend's cock. Tony grabbed Adrien's cock and stroked it. He played with it a bit, feeling it and pulling it gently, then with a slow and gentle gesture he pulled it back revealing a wet acorn.

— Your cock is really beautiful, said Tony.

— You tell me that every time.

— It's because I never tire of it.

Tony leaned down and put the acorn in his mouth to lick it while holding the base of Adrien's cock. He then began to go back and forth on Adrien's sex, making his friend moan.

Not to be outdone, Adrien grabbed Tony's cock and started to jerk him off. With his right hand, he held his friend's cock and observed her as if it was the first time he had seen her. He had never looked at him too much as Tony didn't waste an opportunity to stare at him and touch him.

Tony's cock was smaller than Adrien's, but wider and the glans larger and crenellated at the base. Adrien noticed that when he held her within the width of his hand, only the tip of his cock and the glans protruded.

Adrien felt his friend strive on his cock which he swallowed and sucked with efficiency and desire. Not wanting to be outdone with Tony, he began to jerk him off faster and faster, massaging his testicles with his other hand.

— Oh, you're doing it right, Adrien. You are good, it's so good.

— Glad that it pleases you.

— How are you?

— I won't take long.

— Tell me when you enjoy it so that I can take it all in my mouth.

— Okay.

Adrien was brushing Tony's thick cock, which was chuckling with pleasure. He then wanted to please her. He leaned over to his friend's cock and ran his tongue over it before putting it in his mouth.

In surprise, Tony stopped and watched his friend suck him off.

— Oh thank you Adrien. I was dreaming about it, Tony said before throwing himself more hard on his friend's cock.

With vigor, Tony activated his friend's cock.

Exhilarated, Adrien licked Tony's cock. The taste was nice and he could tell Tony was enjoying it, but his cock was on the verge of exploding. Tony then thrust Adrien's entire cock into his mouth, making his friend cum all at once.

— Aaah, Adrien cried, feeling his spunk pour into Tony's mouth who swallowed everything with the greed of a thirsty.

— Me too, I'm going to cum, Tony warned then.

Adrien pulled his mouth away from Tony's cock and saw his friend burst with pleasure. The semen spurted out of his cock and flowed onto Adrien's hand who felt the hot liquid on his skin. Tony rolled onto his back and thanked Adrien for sucking him off.

— Did you like sucking me off? Tony asked.

— It was a pleasure.

— I'll think about it all night. Finally, there may be hope that you change sides.

— Not yet.

— Don't forget that you promised to bugger me if I keep my job for a month, said Tony before kissing Adrien on the cheek, picking up his things and going to bed leaving Adrien the cock to the air in the living room.

Adrien smiled: his friend hadn't forgotten his promise, but he hadn't told him that in Cannes he had buggered Philippe and that he had liked it.

We'll see, Adrien thought to himself before going to bed too.

The invitation to the general

Adrien was awakened by a cry in the apartment. He jumped up from his bed, put on a pair of boxers, and left the room.

Ludivine was standing in front of the kitchen, her kettle was on the floor. In front of her, Tony, wearing a tight white tank top as his only garment, was drinking coffee with a slice of butter in his other hand. His cock swayed between his legs and he did nothing to hide it.

— What is happening ? asked Adrien.

— He scared me. I hadn't seen he was in the kitchen, said Ludivine.

— I was making myself a slice of butter for my breakfast when I heard him scream behind me, Tony said.

— I didn't know someone else was sleeping here.

— Adrien invited me to spend the night with him, Tony said, scratching his balls.

Embarrassed, Adrien made the introductions before asking his friend to get dressed.

— Usually you don't mind when I'm naked. Don't you want us to have lunch first?

— Don't worry about me, said Ludivine.

She turned her head, refilled her kettle and returned to her desk. Adrien joined Tony in the kitchen to have lunch. They nibbled a bit while looking out the window at the Trocadero gardens.

— It's nice to see some greenery, said Tony, who lived in a tiny attic with only view of the rooftops of Paris.

— It's relaxing, approved Adrien.

Tony made Adrien start to erect by touching his cock. He had always been very tactile.

— I'll give you a morning blowjob, but I'm not sure you'd enjoy it with your assistant in the next room, he said, giving her a wink.

They then went to get dressed and Adrien tidied the living room, clearing away the leftovers from the previous day's meal. He later found Ludivine in the office. She had already turned on her computer and was answering emails. She was very serious with her glasses. Professional, she pretended nothing had happened and asked him for permission to validate the painting work of two apartments. Adrien had taken a look at the quotes the day before, but he couldn't remember the amounts.

— What do you think about it ? he asked.

— You have to do it, otherwise you won't be able to re-let them as is.

— Okay.

Tony joined them shortly after. He had put on tight-fitting, low-rise jeans that he probably wore nothing under and had packed his things into a duffel bag.

— I will let you. It was very nice this movie night. I come back when you want, he said, sending a kiss to Adrien then greeting Ludivine before leaving the apartment.

— It's your boyfriend ? asked Ludivine.

— No, my best friend.

— I thought you were together as he was naked in the kitchen.

— No, we're only friends, said Adrien before pouring out a coffee.

Adrien then thought about his relationship with Tony. He was his best friend, but the latter spent his time making advances and touching his cock. He also enjoyed being sucked by Tony and had also enjoyed tasting his cock. Could their friendship turn into love? Did he want to become gay? These questions had been bothering him for some time, but Adrien also loved girls and he had no intention of not seeing any more.

— And you, your wedding dress? he asked to change the subject.

— Great, I spent the day fitting with my friend, but I ended up finding the dress of my dreams. You want to see her ?

Adrien nodded.

Ludivine took out her cell phone and scrolled through the photos of the fittings. She had put on all the dresses in the store and each time her friend had taken a picture of her. The styles were different and sometimes Ludivine looked like a bag. Finally, she had opted for a long, pleated white dress with short lace sleeves that looked a bit like a Greek goddess, but suited her well.

— I would also have a veil and a braid in my hair. I'm really happy.

— She is very beautiful.

Part of the back was bare and Ludivine had been photographed from all angles. She scrolled through the photos to below chosen for the occasion from a catalog. It was a very daring white lace set with stockings and a body open at the crotch and barely hiding the breasts.

— Oops, there was also an important choice of underwear, said Ludivine, quickly changing the photo.

— These look very good to me, said Adrien, trying to imagine Ludivine with them.

Her future husband would have a pleasant surprise once the dress was removed.

Adrien then tried to delve into the restaurant accounts, but he quickly had a headache. Luckily, he was saved by a call from Maeva, the head of the beauty salon.

Ludivine put the phone on speakerphone and introduced him to Adrien.

— Hello young man. I was associated with your aunt for the management of the two beauty salons that we opened together. She lent me the funds to start my activity.

— Nice to meet you, Adrien greeted her.

— I can't wait to meet you sweetie. Your aunt told me about you.

Adrien was surprised: he didn't think Viviane cared so much for him.

Maeva called to indicate that she was going to buy a new wax heater. The one in the living room had just let go.

— I'll keep my new partner informed, Maeva said softly.

Taking the opportunity, she invited Adrien to come to the show to show him around his shop.

— With pleasure, said Adrien, who had never set foot in a beauty salon.

— And you my little apricot. When do you come for waxing?

— Soon, said Ludivine, blushing.

Maeva then signaled that her next date had arrived. A handsome man to whom she had to make the jersey.

— I have more and more men in my living room. If you want Adrien, I'll make you the jersey. I'll take care of it myself, Maeva said before hanging up.

Maeva had a soft voice, but sounded quite exuberant.

— He's a personality, Ludivine confided. She is very kind and very professional.

— Why is she calling you her little apricot?

— It's a nickname she gave me, said Ludivine embarrassed. His salon "Le Mogai" is in the 13th arrondissement. He's very handsome, you should go meet her. Viviane liked him a lot, said Ludivine while indicating the address.

Maeva and Viviane had also opened a second salon, but Maeva spent most of her time at the Mogai.

Adrien promised himself to discover this profession. His aunt rubbed shoulders with very diverse people, between the notary Delacroix and the esthetician Maeva.

Ludivine then took a square box from her stack of mail and handed it to Adrien. It was an invitation for the general of the last play staged by the Théâtre de la Libellule in the Goutte d'Or district. The general took place this afternoon.

— Members are always invited to attend, as well as at the first performance. Viviane was very fond of the theater and was closely linked to several actors of the company, including the director and director of the theater, Pierre Labrume. They were all at the funeral.

— I don't remember anymore, there were a lot of people.

— Monsieur Labrume is a little man with curly brown hair with glasses and a goatee. He is also a personality.

The description reminded him of a somewhat wacky man Adrien had seen in the apartment before. Dressed in Emmaus clothes, he had struck her as strange.

— I'm going to attend the dress rehearsal, said Adrien.

— Viviane supported the artists she appreciated.

Adrien nodded. Her aunt went out a lot, but she had never spoken to her about art when her apartment was filled with works and paintings.

The Libellule theater

Adrien took the metro to Château Rouge station to get to the Libellule theater. When he got out of the metro, several street vendors offered him cigarettes, but Adrien only smoked occasionally to party and tobacco was bad for his health.

He walked up Boulevard Barbes to Rue de la Goutte d'Or, then took Rue des Islettes to Place de l'Assomoir. The theater was next door in a backyard.

Adrien came to the reception desk and handed his box to a thin woman in her sixties with salt and pepper hair that fell on her shoulders.

— The general has just started, I was going to close. You're the last one, she said, getting up from her seat.

She wore a thin floral dress that hugged her two small breasts without a bra.

— How did you get this box? Have I never seen you here?

— I am Viviane Leguen's nephew.

— I really liked Viviane, we had a good time together, she said before leading Adrien to a performance hall with a hundred seats. About twenty people were in the room and the artists were already on stage.

The teller told her to get into the second row so she could see well as she got into the back. Adrien sat down in the place indicated. He recognized among the spectators an old friend of his aunt who greeted him with a wave of her hand. The general was played with the lights in the room, some actors noticed his arrival.

Adrien sat back in the chair and watched the artists. He no longer remembered the title of the play, but it was an original creation by the director of the theater.

On stage, a black man chanted verses in a Robin Hood-style bow costume with a green cap on his head and a busty blonde woman strolled breasts out. From time to time, she would interrupt the bow, asking him for details on a line or expressing her displeasure. In the background, another blond was busy in a fitted kitchen. A young girl dressed as a Red Riding Hood entered the stage to interact with the bow.

Adrien was not long in being taken by the acting and having a good laugh at times. There was real depth to the lyrics and each actor seemed possessed by their character.

A woman in a long black dress with her face concealed under a hood walked on stage with a scythe and rushed to the bow which she attacked mimicking an execution. With a loud cry, the bow collapsed.

— Who will become the new torchbearer? asked the blonde. Who will fight against ignorance?

— I ! suddenly shouted a voice from behind the scenes.

The director entered the stage, resuming the last tirades of the bow. He wore a black blaser with a white shirt and bow tie, but no pants. His huge cock swayed between her legs. Adrien had never seen one so big. The man had to be proud of his phallus to exhibit it like this. He engaged in a verbal battle with death which eventually left the scene. He approached the bow, picked up his calo and put it on his head.

The curtain closed and the spectators applauded. Adrien imitated them: he couldn't tell if the play was good, but he had had a good time.

The teller told her that there was now a pot with the artists. A table had been set in a corner. Adrien stepped forward. His aunt's friend struck up a conversation with him.

— Adrien, I'm glad to see you here. I hope you will continue to support art like your aunt. It was wonderful.

Adrien knew she was the rich widow of a captain of industry. He had a fruit juice before the black actor joined them and placed a kiss on the hand of his aunt's friend. The director of the theater, Pierre Labrume, who had put on trousers, came to talk to them.

— Jocelyne, who was at reception today, told me that you were Viviane's nephew. Welcome to the Théâtre de la Libellule. I am very happy to see you here.

Pierre offered her his condolences: he too had lost a friend. He then asked Adrien what he thought of the play.

— It was good, I appreciated, but I'm not an expert.

The other artists had joined the pot. The busty blonde had tucked her breasts into her dress, the young chaperone was now wearing leggings and a sweater, the man who had cooked in the back of the stage had not changed. A young woman with brown hair bobbed all dressed in black with a gothic look was toasting one. Adrien understood that it was the one who played death.

The other members were not long in leaving and Pierre gathered the artists around him to present them to Adrien. The busty blonde was called Babeth, the teller Jocelyne, the black man Moussa, the chaperone Sophie, the blond man Allan and the brunette Rachel.

— Viviane was a patron for us. She took charge of many repairs to the theater. Without her, this troop would not be what it is.

All approved. Adrien was a little embarrassed. He didn't know anything about Viviane's artistic activities and didn't like to be the center of attention. Pierre then specified a specific feature of the troop.

— We care a lot about our members and we like to have a special relationship with each of them. This is why at least one artist in the troupe has intellectual and carnal relations with a member. This allows us to create a unique bond with everyone.

Adrien was speechless for a moment, not knowing what to say. Luckily, Pierre continued the explanations.

— I was lucky to have this special relationship with Viviane. I'll talk to you about it occasionally if you're interested. We spent long evenings and nights at his apartment remaking the world, acting and having fun, but I guess I'm not the best person to set up this special relationship with you, said Pierre, stroking himself. the goat.

Around him, the other artists nodded. The situation called for reflection.

The blond man volunteered, but Adrien's face was enough to convince them that this was not a good idea.

— I would like to take care of him, but I already have several members who want to see me outside the theater. I am already taken almost every night and by all the holes. I won't have time to introduce her to our art, said Babeth, the busty blonde.

— You are right, it is not wise, said Pierre.

— I don't mind, said Jocelyne. The best soups are made in old pots.

— But not with new carrots, said Pierre.

The problem seemed insoluble for the assembled artists. Babeth then offered to show Adrien behind the scenes so that they could discuss it among themselves. The busty blonde took Adrien's hand and pulled him behind him. She wore a brown dress that barely concealed her generous curves.

— The theater is not very big.

Backstage, she took him to a room full of costumes from floor to ceiling, in another, sets were grouped together and finally, there were two small rooms that served as a dressing room: one for women and one for women. men.

Babeth brought him into the women's house.

— Come on, I'll take care of you while the others agree. They can be a bit long at times, but they should get along.

— Do all your members sleep with you?

— Sometimes, some with several and we are not against a small orgy on occasion. Your aunt has already received us all in her beautiful apartment. We had fucked like crazy. She knew how to receive: the caterer was great. Do you live there?

— Yes, she left me the apartment.

— In general, we have a privileged relationship with only one member at a time. Pierre takes care of several women and a man. I have five men, some of whom are sacred perverts. They stuff me everywhere and one especially by the back door. It's rare on the weeks when I can sit down without having a sore butt, but I like it too much to stop.

Babeth pushed Adrien against a table and without warning him, she attacked the waistband of his pants and undid his jeans before lowering them, carrying his boxers in his gesture. She then took off the straps of her dress and brought it down to her waist revealing two huge nipples. Without preamble, she knelt in front of Adrien and took his cock in his hand.

Very quickly, Adrien's cock hardened and lengthened.

— I'm going to put her warm between my breasts, she'll be fine there.

— I'm sure of it, said Adrien, letting it go.

Once Adrien's cock was hard, Babeth brought it to her mouth to lick it. She then placed it between her two big breasts and began to masturbate with it.

— Is she there?

— Yes, said Adrien who began to make movements of the pelvis to rub his penis against the artist's breasts.

The feeling was pleasant and exciting. No girl had ever done this to her, but none of her girlfriends had ever had such big breasts.

— Do not hesitate to cum on me, I love it. It makes my chest hot and I love to feel this liquid running down my breasts.

— You're sure ?

— Yes, don't hold back.

She then squeezed Adrien's sex more forcefully between her breasts. The long cock was compressed and swallowed up by the nipples. Adrien loved it.

— Go ahead, said Babeth. I want you to cum on me.

— Yes, I'm not far, said Adrien, his penis drooling on Babeth's chest.

He activated himself: the warm sex stuffed between Babeth's soft and mellow breasts until he felt her juices rise in him and his cock exploding between the actress's breasts.

— Hoaa! Adrien moaned.

Babeth continued to enclose her penis between her breasts, making all the semen that it contained on her chest flow.

— Oh, it's hot. Its good.

Several jets of cum spread over the shells of Babeth who dipped her index finger in it to taste Adrien's juice.

— Um, I smell a little nutty taste.

— I eat a lot of Nutella.

— Too bad I already have too many men to cram me, we would have understood each other.

She patted Adrien's cock on her breasts to squeeze out every last drop then she licked his glans before going to get a tissue to wipe her chest. After cleaning herself, she put her dress back on.

Emptied, Adrien pulled up his pants.

— Did you like it ? asked Babeth.

Adrien nodded.

— So much the better. It was a bit quick. I prefer to be lying on a bed with my partner on top of me and take my time. I'm all wet from what we've just done, said Babeth, touching the fabric of the panties under her dress. If I was not expected, I would ask Moussa or Pierre to smash my pussy with their huge cock. Come on, we'll find them.

Adrien followed her into the auditorium where the discussion seemed over.

— Did you show him around? Pierre asked.

— I showed him the premises and my breasts, said Babeth.

Embarrassed, Adrien ran his hand through his hair, wondering what the troop had decided. Pierre walked up to him and told him about their discussions.

— It will be neither Jocelyne, nor Moussa, nor I who will spend a moment with you. Rachel volunteered.

The brunette with bobbed hair and gothic look winked at Adrien. She was thin and barely shorter than Adrien with green eyes.

— I'll call you when I have a spare moment. I hope you don't do like the last member I took care of. He left the theater after spending the night with me.

— What did you do to her? Adrien worried.

— I told him about my art and we had sex all night, maybe too much for him.

— He was not an art lover. It was a mistake to welcome him among our members, says Pierre. Adrien is Viviane's nephew. He is almost part of the family. He won't leave us.

Adrien exchanged his phone number with Rachel, then he left the theater after thanking the actors for their welcome.

They are nice, wacky, but nice, Adrien said to himself as he walked through the Goutte d'Or district.

The two olives

Before leaving the apartment, Adrien texted Tony to let him know he was at the pizzeria. He had confided to Ludivine the request of his friend and the young woman had advised him to change his appearance so that their story seemed more credible.

— Do I really need these accessories? Adrien had inquired.

— You don't look like gay. When I see Tony, I have no doubts.

Adrien had agreed with Ludivine's advice and had followed her advice. He then took the metro to Saint Paul station in the 4th arrondissement and headed for Place Sainte Catherine a few blocks away. Two blocks away, he tied his aunt's Hermes scarf around his neck, rolled his pants up to mid-calf, put on Chanel No. 5 and put a floral bob on his head. He also carried a leather handbag from his aunt over his shoulder.

When he looked at himself in a store window, he felt ridiculous.

It's for Tony, Adrien said to himself as he walked up the rue d'Ormesson to the little cobbled square lined with trees and benches where the "two olives" pizzeria was located.

Tables were set up on the sidewalk. Inside, Tony, a black apron around his waist and a tray in hand, was serving customers. Adrien was suddenly afraid to enter and had to encourage himself to push open the door and enter the pizzeria. Freezing on the threshold, he didn't know what to do.

Seeing her, Tony nearly dropped his tray. Quickly, he recovered and greeted his friend.

— Adrien, you finally come to see me, he said before placing a kiss on the lips of his supposed boyfriend and slapping him on the buttocks.

— Don't overdo it, Adrien whispered.

— It has to look real, Tony said, leading Adrien to the counter on the right. Behind, a muscular dark-haired man with dark skin officiated. The man in his thirties was called Come and had a little Italian accent. He eyed Adrien suspiciously.

— Behind the stove is Joey, Tony said, gesturing to a fair-skinned man who entered the main room.

Joey wiped his hands on a white apron tied around his waist. Redhead, with numerous freckles on his face, he smiled broadly, showing his white teeth. Tall and strong, he seemed confident.

— Adrien is the love of my life, Tony said after introducing his friend to them.

— He's very cute, Joey said as Come frowned and glared at him.

Adrien easily guessed who the jealous one was causing Tony trouble was.

— We've known each other since childhood with Adrien. It took a while for him to accept me as his boyfriend, but I ended up convincing him and getting my way, Tony said.

— Soon engaged then? Come asked.

— I hope he will ask me quickly, Tony said, hugging Adrien around the waist, causing his friend's embarrassment.

Come offered a drink to Adrien who accepted a blackcurrant lemonade.

— I think I found my place here. I'm fine with Joey and Come, Tony said.

Adrien looked around: the pizzeria looked nice. The decor was neat, red and white checkered tablecloths covered the wooden tables, and an oven was visible in the back of the room. Through the window, we had a breathtaking view of the square. It was relaxing and exotic. We would never have thought we were in the heart of Paris.

Tony took the opportunity to pet his friend. He was radiant. It pleased Adrien to see him happy.

— Your scarf is very beautiful, complimented Joey.

The scarf featured many colors with a strong orange cast. Adrien had chosen it from among his aunt's many scarves.

— I like the scarves, said Adrien.

— I'll give you more, sweetheart, Tony said.

— Joey uses the scarves to tie my hands to the bed before picking me up from behind. He's a real brute, Come blurted out, winking at his companion.

— You never complained about it, said Joey.

— That is true. And you Adrien, do you tie up Tony?

— No.

— You could try, I wouldn't be against it, Tony said. I am ready to do anything to make you happy.

— Love is beautiful, said Joey. It reminds me of our beginnings.

— It's true that we were crazier at the time. We wanted to fuck everywhere. We even did it on the square one night before opening our pizzeria. I think it brought us luck.

Joey then returned to his oven to prepare his ingredients. The first customers were arriving. Tony sat them down at the table and took their orders. Behind the counter, Come was preparing the drinks and handling the cash register.

— Are you more dominant or dominated? he asked Adrien between two orders.

— Uh, dominant.

— Like Joey. I love it when he knocks me down like a beast. He looks very sweet, but in bed he bangs my ass with force and likes to put all kinds of objects in my little hole to punish me when I have been too jealous or unbearable.

Come then confided to him, as to an old friend, some of their intimate games. Embarrassed, Adrien listened to him without saying anything.

— I also like when he ties my cock with a string or a thin rope. I find it very exciting. You should try it on Tony, I'm sure he would like it.

— I'll talk to him about it.

— I'm happy for you, you are a beautiful couple. When I saw Tony arrive, I was a little jealous. I would have preferred a waitress, but I can't refuse Joey a thing.

— Tony cares about this job, he needs to stabilize himself.

— It is true that he looks good here.

Tony went from table to table, taking care of everyone carefully.

— Do you want to eat here?

— No, I planned to go to the Mogai beauty salon. It's not far.

— Do you know Maeva?

— We have already discussed.

— She's super nice and she's the best beautician in the swamp. Once, I asked him to make me a complete to surprise Joey. She made my asshole with tweezers and put cream on my bikini line to make my skin soft like a baby. What type of treatment are you going there for?

— I don't know yet, I'll see.

— You should try their manicure. Look at the wonders she does, Come said, showing her his hands.

Her fingernails were painted black and there was no dead skin at the tips of her fingers. Come seemed very satisfied with the work done.

— The Mogai is an institution in the neighborhood.

Adrien was happy to know that the salon in which he held shares was successful. Between courses, Tony found him to kiss him.

— Soon the room will be crowded and I will not have a minute to myself until the end of the shift.

— I'm going to go, said Adrien, getting up.

Tony gave him one last kiss touching his buttocks and thanked him for stopping by. Adrien greeted Come and Joey and left the pizzeria. At the corner of the next street, he lifted his scarf and bob and stowed them in his purse. There was nothing he could do about the scent, but he was glad he had done Tony a favor.

The Mogai

As he walked through the neighborhood towards Elie Wiesel Temple Square, Adrien received a text from Rachel. The actress invited her to come to her house this evening for her initiation into the theater. There was something appealing about her gothic look that made Adrien accept the invitation before continuing to rue de Bretagne.

The living room was opposite the square. Ever since his aunt had launched him to discover his past, he went from surprise to surprise and met new people. He stared for a moment at the sober brown front of the Mogai. A film covered the windows so that we cannot see inside.

Adrien pushed open the door and entered a fragrant space with soft background music. On the left side, two nail tables had been set up. In one, a shaved-haired brunette in a white blouse was doing a manicure on a woman. On the right side, pink armchairs occupied the space and green plants were arranged in the four corners of the room. Two other clients were waiting. The walls were white except the one on the right which was painted with broad horizontal stripes of red, orange, yellow, green, blue and purple like the flag of the LGBT community.

— Is it for a date? Asked the shaved brunette.

— I'm coming to see Maeva.

— She's in the cabin, have a coffee if you want.

A machine was installed against a wall next to the pink armchairs. Adrien poured himself an espresso then sat down on one of the available chairs. On the coffee table in front of him, magazines were arranged: Stubborn, Friendly, Attitude... Out of curiosity, Adrien took a Friendly.

A hallway with doors led to the end of the living room. A woman and a very effeminate young black man with a pale yellow blouse came out.

— This massage was divine Alioune, said the woman.

The young man accompanied the client to the living room door before leading another to one of the cabins.

The girl at the nail table finished her manicure and called the last client who was waiting.

— Maeva won't be long. I think she does an integral, it's a little longer.

The brunette took a basin out of a cupboard to do a dry hand treatment.

Adrien finished his coffee by observing the place. There was an atmosphere filled with benevolence and serenity in the living room, like a ray of sunshine in the midst of the Parisian gray.

Another cabin door opened and a man in a gray suit stepped out, followed by a tall brunette with long hair curled up to her back. She wore a purple blouse that went down to mid-thigh revealing her long, slender legs and had tied a thin black leather strap around her waist. His features were fine and carefully made up.

— Thank you for everything, said the man to Maeva after settling.

Maeva then turned her attention to Adrien and smiled.

— Are you Viviane's nephew?

— Yes.

— I was a little longer than expected, but he needed to talk. I'm going to take a break, you come with me to the back room.

Adrien put down his magazine and followed Maeva. There was something magnetic about the beautician.

— There are three hair removal booths, said Maeva, opening a door to show Adrien the place. There was a massage table and various devices.

At the end of the living room, she ushered Adrien into a room with a table and a sofa. On the table, a kettle and boxes of tea were placed. Maeva infused a sachet in a mug with her first name while Adrien sat on the sofa.

— I was living here when I opened the living room. I couldn't afford rent and equipment credit.

A small skylight was fixed at the top of the wall. It was the only room that was not repainted. Three lockers were against the back wall.

Maeva took her tea bag out of the mug and threw it in the trash. She sat down on a chair and crossed her long, slender legs.

— My meeting with your aunt changed my life. I owe him a lot. Do you know how we met?

— No, my aunt spoke little of her business to me.

Maeva took out a pack of thin cigarettes and lit one.

— The temple square brought me luck. At the time, I was a home beautician. I had just started and it wasn't working very hard. One day, I passed by the square and I sat down on a bench where an elegant woman was giving breadcrumbs to the pigeons. We started a discussion and she ended up telling me that she had broken a nail. I cut it for him and I did a color touch-up. She wanted to pay me, but I refused. In the end, she asked for my business card, but I didn't have one. She took my number, but I didn't think she would call me back.

These memories plunged Maeva into the past. There was something nostalgic about listening to him speak.

— She had just visited the building where we are and was hesitant to buy it. I found out afterwards. Our meeting decided her to invest in the marsh. She called me back for treatment and recommended me to her friends. I told him about my dream of opening my own salon. Little by little, we hit it off and she offered to move me to the room in the building she had bought.

Adrien then realized that the whole building belonged to him now. He had not yet reviewed the list of possessions his aunt owned.

— Why did she associate with you? She could have just rented the room from you.

— No bank wanted to lend me money. My income was not declared, I had no savings, no property, lived in a poor roommate and I am a transsexual.

This last sentence made Adrien jump. He had finally understood what was different about Maeva and the link with the flag painted on the wall.

— I cried in front of your aunt for not being able to realize my dream. It was then that she decided to partner with me.

Maeva had tears in her eyes. In emotion, she spilled some of her tea on her blouse.

— Damn, she cursed.

She stubbed out her cigarette, undid the leather thong around her waist, and took off her blouse. Just dressed in pink panties with transparent lace, Maeva threw her blouse in the basket and took another from the wardrobe.

She was shaved all over her body and had two small breasts round like little apples. At the level of his sex, a bump deformed his panties and Adrien could see behind the laces, a small hairless man's penis.

Maeva put on a clean purple blouse and left it ajar in front of Adrien for a moment.

— Didn't you know I was a trans before you came? she asked before closing it.

— No.

— Are you disturbed ?

— No.

— I really liked your aunt. She was very open-minded.

— Did you sleep together?

— It almost happened once when we opened the second lounge. We had a drink to celebrate and we kissed, but it didn't go any further. We had too much respect for each other to continue.

— What were your relations?

— Over time, she became my friend and confidante. I was his esthetician and his partner. A little bit at the same time. We intended to expand the Mogai by recovering the room next door which will be released to make a hammam and a real relaxation area.

Maeva also explained to him that the Mogai was a haven for many people in the swamp. Members of the LGBT community could come here without fear and speak without being blamed. These two employees were a lesbian and a gay. She was also involved in many associations and movements.

— And you ? What are you going to do ?

— I am a little lost. I find an aunt that I didn't know and I don't know what to do with my life.

— Why do you smell Viviane's perfume so strongly?

Adrien explained to him what he had done for his friend Tony, which made Maeva laugh a lot.

— Come is very jealous and he has plenty. Joey is a hot bunny chasing every cock in the swamp. Come has been cuckolded for years. You did well to pass yourself off as your boyfriend's boyfriend. Come would have ended up spending his nerves on him.

Hearing that Joey was a flirt, Adrien felt a pang in his heart and worried about Tony. His friend too risked falling in love with Joey and being seduced before being thrown like a used condom.

— Your aunt was the last person I went to for treatment. We waxed together, drinking good wine and eating a good meal that she had ordered from the caterer. It amused him a lot to see my breasts and my cock.

— What was your name before?

— Mathieu, but I changed my first name last year.

Adrien and Maeva discussed Viviane for a long time and Adrien's lack of plans for the moment.

— She asked me to try to get to know her. It's what I'm going to do.

— She was more complex than many people I have met.

— She has always been so distant to me when she had such a full life.

— She loved you very much and wanted to protect you. She also had a lot of pain in her life.

Before leaving, Adrien questioned her about Ludivine's nickname.

— My little apricot, it's very simple. I do a full bikini waxing for her and her penis looks like a cute little apricot. I can't help but admire her every time she comes here.

As she left, Maeva kissed Adrien on the cheek and hugged him. She was delighted to have met him and hoped to see him soon.

— Come back when you want. Alioune will give you a massage. He has golden hands.

— See you soon, said Adrien leaving the living room.

Poetry under the roofs of Paris

In the evening, Adrien went to the address given by Rachel, rue d'Aumale in the 9th arrondissement. He had brought a bottle of wine and bought a bouquet of roses in the colors of autumn. A little nervous, he wondered how this evening was going to be one-to-one with the actress.

Rachel seemed mysterious to him with her gothic look. He rang the doorbell and Rachel told him to go up to the attic after the 6th floor. There was no elevator.

Breathless, Adrien found her in front of her door under the roof.

She was wearing a long black button-down shirt and her legs were bare. A tattoo adorned her left thigh and a salamander adorned her right ankle. Her lips were painted black. A streak of black eyeliner and dark orange eyeshadow made up her green eyes, which appeared luminous in the midst of her bobbed brown hair.

Adrien handed him the bottle of wine and the flowers.

Rachel looked at the wine first.

— Bordeaux, my favorite wine. For the flowers, you shouldn't have, my man is going to give me a shit when he sees them.

— He's there ?

— No, he's on set all week, but he might think it's serious between you and me if he sees flowers. We are a free couple. We have adventures each on our side, as long as it is not regular.

Rachel recognized, however, that the roses were beautiful. She let Adrien in and showed him his home.

She lived under the roof in two attics joined together in a row. It was very small and not very tidy. The first room served as the kitchen and dining room with a small table and two chairs pushed against the wall to make a passage. On the other side, there was a tiny kitchen area and behind a door, Adrien guessed a shower and a toilet. In the other attic, a mattress was placed on the floor and boxes stacked on top of each other were used for storage.

— I prepared raw vegetables to nibble on, I'm not a cordon bleu, Rachel warns, putting the roses in a vase.

She opened the bottle of wine and filled two glasses to toast with Adrien.

— To the new member of the Théâtre de la Libellule.

— Thanks for the invitation.

— I want to respect the customs of the troop. Pierre and the others are keen on it. They like to fuck with the members they like.

— I didn't know you had a boyfriend. I don't want you to be in trouble.

— We have not sworn loyalty and we allow deviations. Before you arrive, my boyfriend sent me a selfie of him with a chubby little girl he plans to fuck tonight. At least you are cute. I think that's all he found in the Poitevin to empty his balls. He is doing a report on the marshes for France 2, he is a cameraman, says Rachel before showing him the photo of an elderly man with a small curly brunette a little strong with thick dark glasses. The man was bearded and much older than Rachel.

— He's older than you.

— We're twenty years apart, but he's not the worst guy I've ever met. Do you want to smoke some weed to relax?

Adrien smoked on rare occasions, but the evening promised to be special too, he let himself be tempted.

Rachel pulled out a small plastic bag containing cannabis buds from a cupboard. She took one which she crushed and mixed with tobacco from a cigarette in the palm of her hand before rolling a joint with two sheets of paper and adding a cardboard filter. Rachel lit the joint and hit it several times before handing it to Adrien.

— She is good.

— It's been a long time since I smoked, I'll quickly get high.

— Who cares, the important thing is to have fun.

Rachel pulled out a platter of sliced vegetables and a jar of chive sauce. It was all she had had time to prepare.

Adrien took a few breaths before handing the joint back to Rachel. His head was already spinning. His face made the young woman laugh.

— For your initiation into our art, I want to read you poems by Arthur Rimbaud and then we'll have sex if you want. Unless you just make sure to fuck and don't give a damn about poems.

— It's perfect.

— Do you know Arthur Rimbaud?

Adrien remembered having read one of these texts in high school in French, but his teacher's lessons were so boring that the texts studied quickly became undrinkable.

— Not really.

— I will read you the poems that I find the most beautiful.

From a shelf attached to the wall, Rachel picked up a worn paperback with many bookmarks inserted. Despite her gloomy demeanor, Rachel now had a smiling face and a real desire to share the poems that were close to her heart.

— We will start with "the sleeper of the valley".

Rachel cleared her throat and put all her passion into declaiming these verses which ended badly enough for the sleeper.

> *It is a green hole where a river sings, Madly hanging rags of silver on the grass; where the sun, from the proud mountain, Shines: it is a small valley which foams with rays.*

A young soldier, open mouth, bare head, And the back of his neck bathed in fresh blue watercress, Sleeps; he is stretched out in the grass under the cloud, Pale in his green bed where the light is raining.

With his feet in the gladioli, he sleeps. Smiling as a sick child would smile, he takes a nap: Nature, rock him warmly: he's cold.

The perfumes do not make his nostril shiver; He sleeps in the sun, his hand on his chest Tranquil. There are two red holes on the right side.

She then continued with "the poor dream".

Perhaps an Evening awaits me Where I will drink quietly In some old Town, And die happier: Since I am patient!

If my pain is resigned If I ever have some gold, Will I choose the North Or the Land of Vines? ... Ah! to think is unworthy

Since it is pure loss! And if I become again The old traveler, Never the green inn Could not be opened to me.

— It's not very happy, said Adrien.
— But it's so deep. Life is hard. Listen to this one "Only for us my heart," said Rachel, more and more passionately.

What for us, my heart, are the sheets of blood and embers, and a thousand murders, and the long cries
Of rage, sobs of all hell overwhelming All order; and L'Aquilon still on the debris;

And any revenge? Nothing ! ... - But yes, all still, We want it! Industrialists, princes, senates, Perish! power, justice, history, down! It's our due. The blood ! the blood ! the golden flame!

Everything to war, revenge, terror, My Spirit! Let's turn in the bite: Ah! come on, Republics of this world! Emperors, Regiments, colonists, peoples, enough!

Who would stir up the whirlwinds of furious fire, Than we and those we imagine brothers? Romance friends: it will please us. We will never work, O waves of fire!

Europe, Asia, America, disappear. Our vengeful march has occupied everything, Cities and countryside! "We will be crushed! The volcanoes will jump!" and the ocean struck ...

Oh ! my friends ! - Sweetheart, for sure, they are brothers: Unknown blacks, if

The young woman put all her heart into it. There was something going on in her as she read these verses.

— The theater is my passion. When I step on the boards, I feel alive while the rest of the time I feel like a shadow in this world. On stage, it's like going through a door to another universe.

Adrien understood what she meant. She was radiant now as she put on a rather dark look.

— Is it the same for the others in the troop?

— Pierre understands me and the others are enthusiasts like me. That's why I feel good with them. I have the impression of creating something unique during our performances, of pushing back the nothingness that surrounds us, of pushing back death.

— It's beautiful what you say, it troubles me unless it's the joint and the wine.

— When I play, I live while I feel myself dying off stage. It's very hard to explain, but that's how I feel.

Adrien would have liked to know these sensations. He perceived that Rachel vibrated when she spoke about her art and he understood that he had never lived until now. He was content to walk through life like a ghost aimlessly while his aunt had lived her life as she saw fit.

Rachel followed up with a few quotes from the poet that made them think.

— I is another.

— It's hard to be yourself in this world and not wear a mask all the time, said Adrien.

— I ask myself questions about my life every day.

Adrien poured them more wine and finished the joint. He was confused and felt himself floating on a small cloud.

— Life is a farce for everyone, quoted Rachel.

— What is the meaning of life ? I intended to be a physiotherapist a few months ago before stopping everything when I inherited from my aunt.

— Why physiotherapist?

— My father was a doctor, I wanted to follow his path, but I was not ranked high enough in the exams to be a doctor. I had to fall back on physiotherapist.

— Don't you miss it?

— No, I wanted to imitate my father, not to create my own path. I chose the easy way.

— I believe I am in hell, therefore I am there. That's what I tell myself some days, especially when I can't play.

— What can my life be like? I don't have a passion like you, wondered Adrien. Nothing motivates me to surpass myself and I don't need anything.

— You have to look in yourself, I think we all have a role to play on this earth. "I am not asking for prayers, with your trust only, I will be happy. "

— How beautiful.

— Rimbaud is the greatest of poets for me.

— I am happy to listen to these works with you.

— And me to share them with you.

Without another word, Rachel threw herself on Adrien and kissed him. She sat down on her knees and ran her hands through Adrien's hair.

— I feel good with you, said the actress.

— Me too.

— I'll suck you off.

— You don't have to.

— I want it. I only do this when I feel good and it's pretty rare.

Rachel took a sip of the wine as Adrien took off his pants and boxers and sat back down in the chair. She knelt in front of him, grabbed his cock and brought it to her mouth. Adrien's cock stiffened quickly under the licks of the gothic. She didn't have Tony's technique, but she put her heart into it.

— It's longer than my man's, she said before trying a deep throat that she could not succeed.

With both hands, she gripped Adrien's cock and jerked it off while talking to him about her love for poetry.

— I'm glad you like Arthur Rimbaud. Do you like what I do to you?

— That's great.

— I will continue to suck you, but I do not want you to cum in my mouth. Promised?

— Okay, I'll let you know.

Rachel resumed pumping Adrien energetically. Drool was dripping from her mouth, but Rachel was not paying attention. She wanted to make Adrien come. Through his half-opened shirt, Adrien saw Rachel's small breasts with pierced nipples.

— I'm coming, said Adrien.

Immediately, Rachel withdrew her mouth and jerked off Adrien who soon began to ejaculate. A long jet of cum squirted out and crashed into Rachel's black shirt.

— How good, moaned Adrien satisfied.

— I'm glad you liked it. It was good for me too, but I don't like to swallow. I find the taste foul.

— I understand.

— When I suck my mate, he never warns me. It annoys me, Rachel said, wiping her shirt.

Adrien saw that Rachel was confused and probably excited to have given him a blowjob.

— You want me to make you a cuni?

Rachel looked at him with surprise and envy.

— Would you do that to me?

— Why not ? You just sucked me off, I can lick you well.

— My mate never wants. It's nice.

— It's normal and in addition I like to do that.

Rachel seemed touched. She offered to get into bed. They went into the next room where the mattress on the floor took up all the space. Rachel lifted her stained shirt and slid her black boxers to the floor. As Adrien had perceived, she was not wearing a bra and her breasts, round like apples, had pierced nipples. Her skin was pale and adorned with several tattoos. A large circle with patterns was drawn on her upper back, an arrow on her forearm, and a dragon with a rose covered her upper right thigh and stomach. At the level of his pubis, his fleece was cut with care, forming a brown down.

Rachel lay down in the middle of the bed, put her head on a pillow and spread her legs revealing a long slit. Her lips were thin.

Adrien got naked in turn and lay down in front of Rachel's wet cock. He stroked her pubic hair, then gave her the first lick from bottom to top of the slit to the clitoris.

— Are you sure you don't mind? Rachel asked.

— No.

— Great, I love it. The rare times it was made to me, it was really good.

Rachel closed her eyes and focused on what was going on with her sex. Adrien licked her slit then lingered on her clit with little licks. He put his hands on Rachel's thighs, who was starting to moan. He then inserted his tongue into Rachel's cock and licked it as deep as possible.

— Oh yes, go ahead, continue, Rachel pleaded.

Gently, Adrien massaged her clitoris as he thrust his tongue into Rachel's vagina, whose entire body was now in spasms. Rachel's cock was wet and Adrien was licking it velvety. Sensing Rachel coming, he then attacked her clit until it exploded.

— Hiii! Rachel shouted, releasing a small stream of liquid into Adrien's head and writhing in pleasure on the bed.

Her slender body gasped and when she looked at Adrien she had tears in her eyes.

— I love to be licked, it was great.

Adrien wiped his face with his t-shirt. Rachel had cum inside her head and the sheets were wet at her crotch.

— It's the best night I've spent in a long time. Shall we smoke another joint?

Adrien nodded even though he was already quite stoned.

Rachel went to look for her bag of weed and rolled a firecracker which she handed to Adrien before also bringing back the bottle of wine and chips. She slipped under the duvet and invited Adrien to join her.

— I changed the sheets before you arrived.

Adrien sat down next to him and gave the joint back to Rachel who pulled on it for a long moment, remaining silent, lost in thought. A smile graced her lips as her face was usually frowning.

— I'm sorry to have cum inside your head. It went up suddenly and I couldn't help myself. It's rare that I come like that.

— It's nothing, said Adrien, drinking a little wine.

— My companion did it to me once and it sucked while I love it.

— You want me to start again afterwards?

— Would you do it again? It's so sweet, Rachel said, pulling on her joint.

She leaned over to Adrien and threw the smoke into his mouth before kissing him.

— We'll have sex instead. I want your cock. It's longer than my friend's, I want to see the difference. It's been a while since I have had an adventure while he is not shy.

— As you wish.

— I'm happy to spend a moment with you, you're really nice. The other member I had met was a big jerk. He left the theater after spending the night with me. Viviane's nephew is a good plan.

— Did you know my aunt?

— Very little. I never went to the parties she gave in her apartment, but it was something it seems.

— Tell me.

Rachel handed the joint to Adrien and grabbed her glass of wine before starting to speak.

— Vivianne gave big parties in her apartment with other members and members of the troop who wanted to participate. I only joined the Compagnie de la Libellule for two years and I could not go to the only party organized by Vivianne. It seems his apartment is huge?

— Sixteen rooms in the 16th arrondissement. I've been living there for a few weeks.

— It's a dream compared to here.

Although the attics formed a cocoon, the place was very small.

— Each room must be bigger than your apartment.

Rachel told her what she knew about Vivianne's receptions. Each time, a sumptuous buffet was ordered from a caterer. The actors often improvised a few scenes and at the end, everyone had sex together. Everyone was going to fuck in the bedrooms or on the sofas. Pierre and Moussa loved the atmosphere of these evenings.

— Didn't you know?

— No, but I understand why even in high school I still sometimes went to sleep with a babysitter. When I returned, I had the impression that everything was not in the same place.

Rachel tugged on the joint, listening to Adrien talk about his aunt. She too discovered the character from another angle.

— For Pierre, Vivianne was a goddess. It was class incarnate. Everything he liked about a woman.

— I keep meeting people who admired her and I'm the only one who doesn't know her or only know a tiny part of her life.

— In any case, your cuni was divine.

Adrien took the joint despite his head spinning. In his brain, some neurons could no longer connect, but he felt good with Rachel. He found her beautiful despite her gothic look.

Rachel then slipped a hand under the duvet and touched Adrien's penis which began to harden.

— Already, she wondered. Usually, it takes my man several hours to get it hard again.

— I think it's because I like you.

— It's cute. Blow me a blow gun.

Adrien put the rest of the joint upside down in his mouth and Rachel put her hands around Adrien's mouth who gently blew the smoke into her mouth. Rachel sucked in everything before collapsing on the mattress.

— I'm high, she laughed.

— Me too, said Adrien, crushing the joint.

— Fuck me. I have to fuck when I'm in this state.

She pushed the quilt aside and slipped over Adrien, kissing him and scratching his chest. Adrien ran his hands all over Rachel's body, focusing on her tattoos.

— I like your penis, it's long and thin. I want to feel it in me, said Rachel, rubbing against Adrien's cock, who was stiffening.

She put him inside her and straddled him with her last strength. Wiggling over, she wanted to feel Adrien's cock deep inside her as he stroked her buttocks. Attracted by Rachel's pierced nipples, Adrien straightened up and kissed them.

— Take over, Rachel said, sliding to the side. Come and stuff me, my head is spinning to climb on you.

Without being asked, Adrien came over Rachel and put his cock in her pussy, pushing it inside her all the way to the end.

— Oh, yes, Rachel blurted out.

Adrien then began to inflict powerful blows of the tail and Rachel put her legs around his waist moaning.

— Go ahead ! Keep on going !

Adrien kissed her and stuffed her with all the energy she had left until Rachel cried out in pleasure, releasing a small stream of liquid again.

Adrien sank into her a few more times and cum on her stomach before collapsing beside her.

— You could have let go of me inside, I'm taking my precautions.

— The next time.

Rachel wiped her stomach before whispering in Adrien's ear that he was a great shot.

— My man never made me spend a night like this.

Adrien was swimming. Rachel had exhausted him and he wasn't used to having high sex. The sensations were different and stranger.

— I am dizzy.

— Me too. It is time to sleep. We will continue your initiation into the theater tomorrow.

— I love the theater.

Rachel turned off the light and it wasn't long before they fell asleep.

A cafe at the Louvre

After a morning kiss and a black coffee, Adrien and Rachel promised to meet again soon.

— We still have a few rehearsals for Pierre's new play and I'm doing extras in a restaurant to pay the rent. I'll call you whenever I have a moment. Will you come to the premiere at the end of the week?

— I'll try.

— I want to continue to read you poems and to send me in the air with you. We will change poet next time.

Rachel placed a kiss on Adrien's lips and walked him to the door. Adrien left the building. His mind was still a little fractured from having smoked, but he was well in the freshness of Paris.

He decided to walk the streets. He didn't have any obligations and wondered what other encounters he was going to have while trying to get to know his aunt's life. He had enjoyed the time spent with Rachel. Gothic was not unhinged its charm with these poems.

He walked up to the Louvre pyramid. He liked to observe this glass pyramid which protruded from the ground and inserted itself in the middle of older buildings. The paving stones were damp.

Adrien settled down at the Marly café to enjoy the view of the pyramid while having a breakfast consisting of coffee and pastries which he ate while thinking of Rachel.

Her aunt had tried to introduce her to culture, to take her to the theater and museums, but each time it had been a failure. He had closed and she had thrown in the towel.

I wasn't ready and I didn't want to, Adrien said to himself.

He had always been a good student, but he had never gone beyond. He had never sought to learn more than the minimum provided by the school system. However, he felt that these meetings and Viviane's past were changing him, making him discover the world from another angle.

He then got a call from Tony.

— Hi Adrien, I have a problem. I have to leave my apartment. The owner collects it at the end of the week. I have to find myself a fallback. You can help me out for a few days while I'm looking for something else.

— No problem, the apartment is big. We will not be walking on two feet.

— Great, you saved my life. I start to bring my things this afternoon. I can take your old room if I can't sleep with you.

Adrien smiled and nodded: Tony was incorrigible. His coffee finished, Adrien continued his walk in Paris. He walked through the Tuileries Gardens and observed three ducks frolicking in the water of a pond.

Not being in a hurry, he crossed the Seine via the Pont de la Concorde. He walked along the banks of the Seine to the Eiffel Tower before joining the Trocadéro gardens. When he found his apartment, the morning was almost over and Ludivine was leaving for lunch.

— I worried not to see you.

— I didn't sleep there last night.

Ludivine did not ask a question and gave her an update on the various calls and letters received.

Adrien told him that Tony would sleep here for a few days while he found another apartment.

— It might last. He seems to like you a lot and not just like a friend.

Adrien nodded: he knew Tony's feelings against him and knew the troubleshooting might drag on, but he didn't mind. Tony had always been there for him and he wasn't going to leave his friend on the streets.

— I hope I wouldn't see him walking around naked in front of me, said Ludivine.

— All right my little apricot, said Adrien, winking at him.

— Maeva told you why she called me that, Ludivine guessed, blushing. I'm going to kill her.

Adrien told her about his meeting with the beautician and asked Ludivine what other people Viviane frequented.

— She liked going out and saw people from very different backgrounds, but she had also compartmentalized her life.

— Did you know she had parties with theater artists here?

— I ordered the caterer and I was often entitled to a day off while everything was put away. Do you want me to bring in a cleaning lady? Dust begins to accumulate.

— I'll manage, even if it's much bigger than my two-room apartment.

— I'll help you, suggested Ludivine. You also have to obtain a license.

— I don't know which one to pass. It no longer interests me.

— We'll look together if you want.

Ludivine then spoke to her about her wedding preparations. She had to go with her friend Solène to a candy store to choose the color and the packaging.

Ludivine was a dedicated and invested assistant who tried to help her as best she could. Adrien understood why Viviane had chosen her.

Tony's arrival

In the late afternoon Tony arrived with heavy plastic shopping bags containing his things at the apartment. Adrien helped her carry the bags to her old room.

— You save my life, Tony said. Since I didn't have a lease, this motherfucker owner left me until the end of the week to go.

— There is room: sixteen pieces for two, that should be fine.

— Plus your assistant.

— She's not sleeping there.

Adrien's things were still there in the cupboards. The young man had forgotten that he had left some here when he left.

Tony looked at what was there and discovered a red and black checked lumberjack shirt, a loose sweater that was popular in their teenage years...

— You can leave me your clothes. Even though they're a bit tall, I could still put them on for a fancy dress party.

— I'll take everything back. You will manage with your business.

Tony then approached Adrien and kissed him on the mouth before sticking to him, hugging him.

— You really are my best friend. What will I do without you?

— I wasn't going to leave you on the street.

With tears in his eyes, Tony kissed her again.

— I won't bore you, he promised. I would make myself as small as possible.

— It would surprise me of you and stop fondling my ass. We're not at the pizzeria, said Adrien, who had both Tony's hands on his buttocks.

— Oops, I could lick your ass if you prefer, Tony said, winking at him. I'm as good as carving a pipe.

— I don't want you to approach my anus.

Tony began to put his things in the cupboard under Adrien's gaze. Carefully, he placed his clothes, sometimes folding them up. Tony had a lot of clothes: that's where he spent most of his money. Carefully, he pulled out thongs and lace boxers.

— How's it going at the pizzeria?

— Much better since you've been here. Côme leaves me alone, he almost became a friend. We are much more complicit.

— Maeva told me that Joey was a runner and that Como had been cuckolded for years. Joey isn't after you?

— I already had an affair with him some time ago. He's a bully in bed. He goes like a savage, but there is something sexy about him. That's why Joey offered me the job.

— Como knows?

— Especially not. Como suspects that Joey is cheating on him, but he doesn't know about all of his man's deviations. I even feel sorry for him, he loves Joey so much that he has to close his eyes.

— What about you with Joey?

— It's over and I will not put the table back, even if he has tried a few approaches. I know Como now and I am in a relationship and very much in love.

Adrien burst out laughing. He was relieved that his friend wasn't in the grip of a runner. At least Joey wouldn't break his heart.

With his things packed, Tony thanked his friend once again.

— I'll help you move the rest. Viviane had a car, it will be more practical than public transport.

— I would have stayed for a hug, but I have to go take my shift.

Adrien accompanied him to the door.

— By the way, you remember your promise. Only three days left and I will be at the pizzeria for a month. I'll take my day off so you can bugger me all night long.

Adrien choked: his friend had not forgotten.

— Go away, otherwise you will be late and you risk losing your job.

— Don't worry, I won't pass up such a great opportunity to get fucked by you, Tony said as he left.

Adrien remained alone in the apartment. Tony's presence might change their relationship and he hoped his friend wouldn't be pushy. Even though he liked being sucked off by Tony and he was probably going to fuck him to please him, he wasn't going to give up on girls. He had enjoyed the night spent with Rachel and wanted to see her again.

He walked past the still closed door and tried to turn the handle to no avail.

I wonder what's behind it. Another facet of Viviane that I don't know, Adrien thought to himself, starting to like his aunt.

Ludivine and Tony

Adrien was roused from his sleep by bursts of laughter. He had gone to bed late after watching the first episodes of a new series on Netflix and Tony had woken him up on the couch when he got home at over 1am.

He stood up and put on a pair of jogging pants and a t-shirt.

Two people were talking and laughing in the office. Ludivine, sitting in her chair, her mug in her hand, chatting with Tony standing in black lace-up boxers and a white t-shirt.

— Hi Adrien, Ludivine offered me a coffee with the Riviera and Bar. It is much better than the kitchen pod.

— Do you want one ? asked Ludivine.

Adrien nodded. He was worried that things would go wrong between the two, but Tony and Ludivine seemed to get along well.

Ludivine handed Adrien a cup.

— Ludivine told me about these wedding preparations. I would like to get married too. Once, I went to the ceremony of two friends, it was very moving.

— I'm afraid I'll never be ready on time. Yesterday, I also went with Solène, my best friend, to a stationery store to choose my cardboard box, but I cannot make up my mind and my future husband is not of any help to me.

Ludivine took out of her bag several colored boxes with different stylized writings. The choice seemed difficult.

— Which one do you prefer ? she asked.

Adrien and Tony each pointed to one, but Ludivine hesitated between two others.

— And for the party, you found it? Tony asked.

— I am still searching. This weekend, we will go to see rooms outside of Paris in small castles and converted farms.

— Me, I put my day off to celebrate my first month of work with Adrien. It's one of the first jobs I keep for so long.

— Seriously! cried Ludivine who was already worried about what she would do at the end of her contract with Adrien.

— Yes, I like to change. I never managed to fix myself.

— And me, I never had to work, said Adrien. Apart from a little job at Mac Donald for a few months. It was my aunt who paid me everything.

— My future husband doesn't want me to stay at home, I have to make a living, he doesn't want to support me.

— He looks rude, Tony said. If I married Adrien, I would love him to support me and I will spend my time taking care of him.

Tony finished his coffee, gave Adrien a kiss on the cheek and went to shower. A few minutes later, Adrien and Ludivine heard him sing under the water jet.

— Your pot is funny.

— Glad you got along.

— He came to ask me for advice on a manicure. I think he will stay here for a while.

— Unless there is a companion with an apartment.

— I think it's you he loves.

Just dressed in a towel, Tony walked down the hall, triggering laughter from Ludivine and Adrien.

— You received an invitation for a gallery opening this evening. Your aunt has already bought several works there.

— Tonight is the premiere of the new play by the Théâtre de la Libellule troupe. I promised to go.

The first one

In the evening, well dressed, Adrien went to the premiere of Pierre Labrume's new play at the Théâtre de la Libellule. He had put on a white shirt, pulled out his best jacket and put gel in his messy brown hair.

— Good evening Adrien, greeted Jocelyne at the counter. I'm glad you came.

— I really wanted to see the play again.

— You should have come with friends. Members can take one person with them to each performance.

Adrien entered the room and took the second row like the last time. He wanted to see Rachel again.

On stage, the curtain was drawn. The hall was filling up little by little, but there were still places left when the performance began.

They don't even manage to fill in for the first one, said Adrien.

He himself would never have come if he hadn't been interested in Rachel and a theater associate. Competition from Netflix and consoles was very damaging to performing artists.

The room went dark and the play began. Moussa entered the stage in his Robin Hood costume and declaimed his text on the collapse of the world. Allan, at the back of the stage, was making an omelet in the kitchen decor.

Rachel then appeared in her death costume. Dressed in a long black dress with a hood, she moved silently on stage, like a shadow, sometimes stopping to listen to Moussa, before resuming her furtive walk on the boards.

Adrien couldn't see her face, barely a tip of his hands sticking out of the sleeves of her dress to hold the scythe she was wearing.

— Oh drama of this world, nobody listens to me. Have all become deaf to the words of the last torchbearer? Moussa declaimed.

Adrien could now perceive the subtleties and the messages hidden behind Labrume's text.

Babeth came on stage in turn. Her dress was open and her huge breasts were showing. At first, she wandered aimlessly on stage like a lost soul, then she gradually approached the torchbearer and a discussion ensued. Babeth's face grew worried. She understood part of the torchbearer's message, but not all of it.

Death reappeared on stage and revolved around them.

Adrien caught a glimpse of the lower face of Rachel for a moment, smiling.

The play continued until Rachel's execution of Moussa and the arrival of Pierre Labrume, sex in the air, to take over the role of torchbearer.

Adrien thought he should have brought Tony so that he could see the size of Pierre Labrume's phallus.

The curtain fell and, like one man, the spectators rose to applaud. The room had rained. The actors returned to greet the audience three times. Rachel had taken off her dress. Her face sweating with sweat, she was radiant. She was still dressed in black with dark makeup, but her features were relaxed.

Adrien then remembered her words: she felt alive on stage and it showed.

The spectators left the room except for a few who were waiting for the actors. Some knew each other and discussed with each other. They had planned to go eat together at a couscous nearby.

Pierre arrived first and asked him if he liked the play.

— Even more than during the general.

Pierre was happy. It wasn't long before the other artists arrived after changing, only Rachel was missing.

— Hi Adrien, are you coming with us? asked Babeth.

The blonde whose busty forms stretched the fabric of her dress, had tied a scarf around her throat and put on a waistcoat.

— Rachel's not here.

— She has already left to join her companion who is participating in a conference at the radio house. Did you want to see her?

— I wanted to say hello.

Babeth looked at him questioningly before warning him.

— Rachel's life is complicated and so is she.

The artists and the last spectators set off. Babeth told them she would join them after she finished talking to Adrien.

— Rachel has a lot of quality, but it's often chaos in her head. It is difficult to follow her. His thoughts are often as orderly as the lines of a mad poet.

— I enjoyed the time spent with her listening to poems.

— And when you fucked?

Embarrassed, Adrien nodded before confirming that he had really enjoyed the night spent with him.

— His companion must have learned it and made a scene for him even if they want to be free, especially him. That must be why she left like an arrow at the end of the play. The time with you was good for him, but he's a toxic man.

Adrien was disappointed: he would have liked to chat with Rachel for a while, to hear from her.

In front of him, Babeth was smiling, amused by the look he was making.

— I would like to show you something in the dressing room, she said, taking his hand and leading him into the small room where he had come on her breasts the first time he came to the theater.

Without warning him, Babeth took off her waistcoat, her dress and slid her panties on the floor, finding herself naked in front of Adrien.

— Since the last time I saw your cock, I want you to shove me like a slut. I'm still super horny after a performance and got wet as soon as I saw you. Forget Rachel for a moment and fuck me.

Babeth threw herself on Adrien and kissed him, crushing her busty forms on him. Adrien couldn't help but knead her plump buttocks. With one hand, he stroked her buttock and with the other one of her big breasts, while kissing her.

Babeth opened his shirt for him to feel his skin against her and then attacked the waistband of his pants to catch his cock.

— I think about your cock since you came on me. You won't leave here until you put it deep in me.

Adrien lowered his pants and his boxers and found himself buttocks in the air, while Babeth threw himself on his already hard cock. She moved back to the table and sat there before drawing Adrien towards her by pulling him by the tail and directing the latter's penis towards his crotch.

— Fill me up, she asked.

Without being asked, Adrien entered her and thrust his cock inside her. Her pussy was already wet and slippery. He entered without difficulty and began to kick her cock.

— How good it is, Babeth moaned. Go all out.

Without any preliminary, Adrien stuffed her pussy: Babeth seemed insatiable. She scratched Adrien's chest and insulted him at the same time. She bowed on the table and began to massage her clitoris at the same time as Adrien penetrated her and soon began to enjoy pleasure.

— Ha, thank you Adrien. I wanted too much, she let out the convulsed body of spasms.

After a few more strokes, Adrien came inside her and let his cum spill between her thighs.

— I feel your sperm flowing in me.

Swimming, Adrien sank into a chair to catch his breath. Babeth was panting, happy and sweating. She then took a sheet of paper towel and wiped her penis dripping with cum.

— I regret having already too many lovers, otherwise I would have taken care of you for your initiation into the theater. A little youngster with a long tail, you can't refuse. You have a good kidney stroke.

— You're not bad too.

— I'll go join the others. There are three of my lovers among them. Tonight I'm going to ask them to take me at the same time. One in each hole, it will do me good.

Babeth loved sex and wanted more.

— Aren't they jealous?

— They would like to have me just for themselves, but alone, they will not be able to satisfy me. I love cock too much, but I promise you that when they all put their cocks on me at the same time, I will have a little thought for you, especially when they cum on me. Unless you make sure to come too?

— I'll go home.

— I'll tell Rachel you came by. Call her and suggest something romantic or unusual that will change her from her asshole companion, said Babeth, getting dressed.

Once dressed, she accompanied Adrien to the exit of the theater and rushed to join her friends. Adrien found himself alone in the street and decided to walk home while considering what he could suggest to Rachel to see her again.

The evening with Tony

The next day, while Tony was preparing their evening together, Adrien walked in the gardens of the Trocadero admiring the fountains. He had agreed to celebrate his friend's first month at work and fuck his ass despite his fear that it would change their relationship. He cared a lot about Tony as his best friend and didn't want him to delude himself. He would never give up girls for himself.

From the gardens, it had a breathtaking view of the Eiffel Tower. It was very beautiful and it would undoubtedly be even more beautiful when the bridge which linked the Trocadéro gardens to the Eiffel Tower was pedestrianized and vegetated.

When Adrien returned to the apartment, the lights were out. Candles were lit and incense sticks were burning.

— I'm almost ready, Tony said from his bedroom.

Adrien took the opportunity to shower and put on clean jeans and a white shirt. His friend went out of his way to give him a pleasant evening. He had to play the game. He perfumed himself with his Gentleman de Givenchy and went into the living room.

Candles were burning on the coffee table. A bottle of wine was waiting in an ice bucket and appetizers were placed on the table. Tony had chosen peanuts, olives and appetizers: everything Adrien liked. He sat down on the sofa and waited for his friend.

— I'm ready, Tony said.

Adrien turned around and saw his friend in a different light.

Tony had done makeup. Lipstick adorned her mouth, far colored her cheeks, a line of eyeliner surrounded her eyes and mascara had been put on her lashes. Her brown hair was styled back instead of peak, and long gold curls hung from her ears.

He wore a very short denim shorts revealing his thin shaved legs and a black blouse half open with a wide collar with short sleeves of woman and black ballet flats. Her nails were the same color as her lipstick, and a necklace hung from her neck.

— Do you like me?

— I've never seen you like this.

— It's for special occasions.

— You are very sexy.

Tony walked over to the sofas. He seemed intimidated, uncomfortable when he was usually exuberant and uncomfortable.

Adrien took the bottle of Chardonay and served them two glasses.

— Thank you, Tony said, touching Adrien's fingers as he took the glass. I am very happy to share this evening with you and to be here.

— Me too. You are my best friend and I will never let you down.

— Not this evening.

— Tonight you're my boyfriend too, Adrien said leaning over Tony and kissing him on the mouth.

— Adrien, I dreamed of it, Tony said with tears in his eyes. A romantic evening with you.

Tony put the 2cellos to background music, two talented cellists who revisited the greatest titles with their instrument. While having an aperitif, Adrien and Tony chatted like a couple who spend an intimate moment and confide their desires and their secrets.

— Your coming to the pizzeria changed my relationship with Como. He found you very beautiful and very nice. Since he knows I'm stuck, he's been a lot friendlier to me.

— So much the better.

— I feel good with them even if Joey is sometimes not very cool with Como.

Adrien told Tony about his encounters since he had gone to explore his aunt's past. Tony knew the Mogai by reputation. Maeva had had a rather dissolute life before settling down. Tony never imagined that she could be related to Viviane.

Adrien then told him about the Dragonfly troop whose members slept with their members.

— You've already had two actresses.

— One threw himself on me and the other takes care of my initiation.

— Which one do you prefer ?

— They are very different from each other, Adrien said, describing Babeth and Rachel to him.

Knowing his friend, Tony guessed that Adrien had a thing for Rachel.

— Tonight, you're mine. Don't forget that, Tony reminded him, leaning over to kiss him.

He suggested that Adrien take a selfie to immortalize their evening. The two friends hugged each other and took pictures of each other. Adrien was happy to see his friend so happy.

They then went to table. Tony had set the cutlery and found a silver candlestick in a cupboard and lit the candles to create an intimate atmosphere. He then left for the kitchen to cook a piece of red meat and return with two plates.

He had prepared a piece of romsteck for Adrien with fries and salad. He was a vegetarian. He also opened a bottle of red wine to accompany the meat.

— You spoil me, said Adrien.

— I love you. Anything that pleases you pleases me, Tony said, blowing Adrien a kiss.

Adrien grabbed a knife and attacked his piece of meat. Her evening with Tony was very romantic. He had never had it like this with a girl and discovered his friend from a different perspective. He knew Tony was very sensitive, but he never would have imagined him so caring in the privacy.

At this moment, the door intercom bell rings.

Adrien opened the front door and let a delivery man upstairs. He was surprised to find himself facing Como.

— A very hot pizza, I hope I'm not late.

— Just in time, Tony said coming back from the kitchen.

— You are very handsome, said Como.

— Thank you.

— Have a good evening, said Como, handing the box over to Adrien before leaving.

They returned to the table. Tony had cleared the plates and put on small dessert plates.

Adrien opened the box and found a Nutella pizza with a banana cut in half and rings around it.

— I told Como that it was a special evening for us, so he wanted to offer us dessert.

— It's nice.

Without delay, they cut themselves two large portions which they devoured while dividing the banana.

— I'm stuck, said Adrien.

— I hope you have some strength left to take me from behind.

— Wait till I digest first.

Tony made them two coffees. They settled on a couch and Tony snuggled up to Adrien.

— I dreamed of an evening like that.

— It's a beautiful evening, said Adrien who was struggling to recognize his friend under the makeup.

Tony was getting cuddly and sensual.

— I have never spent such an evening with one of my former companions. All they wanted was to fuck me and shoot themselves.

— I will never let you down, even if I probably don't love you the way you want to.

— How beautiful Adrien, Tony said before leaning in and kissing him.

Adrien kissed him back and their tongues mingled. Tony slid his hand over Adrien's pants and stroked his cock through the fabric. Adrien ran his hand through his friend's hair and kissed him back. Tonight Tony had something different.

Tony undid a button on Adrien's shirt and ran his hand over his chest.

— Are you ready to go further?

Adrien nodded and they went to his room. Tony opened his black shirt and dropped it to the floor. He lifted his ballet flats and slid his shorts onto the floor, ending up in a white thong. Modestly, he put his hands in front of her nipples.

— Do you like me?

— Yes.

Adrien took off his shirt and Tony undid the waistband of his pants to run his hand through Adrien's boxers while kissing him. He slid his clothes over her ankles before kneeling in front of him and sucking him gently.

Adrien felt the warmth of his friend's mouth on his cock and his tongue working on his penis.

— Let's get on the bed, Adrien said lifting Tony up and kissing him.

He stripped off his clothes and joined Tony who was lying on his back. With a gentle gesture, he stroked his friend's hairless chest then ran his hand through his thong and touched his penis. Tony's cock was already drooling with desire. Adrien removed it and kneaded it sensually.

— That's good, Tony moaned.

— Tonight, it's from behind if you still want it.

— I'm waiting for that.

Adrien's cock was already at attention. Tony then got on all fours on the bed. Adrien took off his thong and discovered a purple butt plug in Tony's buttocks.

— I put it in the ass at the beginning of the meal to relax my anus. Like that, you will be able to penetrate me without difficulty and enter me like butter.

— You did that for me?

— So that this evening is perfect.

Adrien was touched by his friend's attention. He had also planned some lube just in case, but with a plug in his ass for over two hours, Tony's anus had to be relaxed.

Adrien grabbed the plug and gently pulled it out. He was over ten centimeters and stretched in length. As a precaution, he put lubricant on his penis and on Tony's washer which was already wide open.

— You're ready ? asked Adrien.

— More than ever.

Adrien placed his penis at the entrance to Tony's buttocks on all fours and his cock penetrated inside his friend's ass without forcing. His cock was sucked into the narrow duct.

— Come on Adrien, come inside me, said Tony.

— I arrive.

Adrien positioned himself and began to introduce his penis into Tony without any difficulty.

— Put it all in all at once, Tony pleaded.

— As you wish.

Adrien sank into Tony until he stumbled against those buttocks. His cock had entered his friend by itself. It was the first time this had happened to him.

— That's good, said Tony.

— It is just beginning.

Adrien then activated in Tony's buttocks. First with small strokes of the pelvis, then with more and more force, tearing cries of pleasure from his friend.

— I knew I would like your long, thin cock. She fits perfectly into me, we are made to fuck together.

— It is true that I did not force.

His cock was good in his friend's butt. It was as if she had found her place. She was warm in the narrow duct and paced back and forth as she pleased.

Tony was moaning with pleasure asking Adrien to bang harder and faster in his ass.

To please his friend, Adrien didn't hold back and sank as deep as possible into Tony. He then reached his left hand towards Tony's cock and squeezed it in the palm of his palm, polishing it, while activating himself in his friend's buttocks.

— Oh yes, keep going. It's so good, Tony pleaded.

Adrien jerked Tony off while stuffing his anus. In his hand, he could feel Tony's cock stretched to the extreme. Beneath him, Tony squirmed on the verge of succumbing. His agony was not long. A powerful jet of cum gushed from her cock and Tony cried out in joy.

— Ha! I enjoy. Oh, yes Adrien.

Adrien fisted a few more punches in that ass before letting his cum spill into Tony's ass.

— Me too, I enjoy.

— Put it all in my ass.

— It's all gone," Adrien said, gently withdrawing and dropping down beside Tony.

— I've never come so hard, Tony said with his cock wet.

Adrien touched her cock, making his friend jump: his cock was wet and soft. Tony had emptied himself on the quilt.

— I'm glad you liked it, Adrien said kissing Tony.

— Thank you for this evening, it is one of the most beautiful of my life.

— Me too, said Adrien moved. He had just had an amazing time with Tony.

— I loved what you did to me.

— It made me curious to see you dressed like this. It changed you. I found you beautiful and exciting.

— Did you like buggering me?

— Yes.

— Then we can start over as many times as you want. If you want I'll put on dresses and make up and we have sex all night long, Tony said looking at Adrien with emotional eyes.

— With pleasure, said Adrien who now had strange feelings for Tony. He saw his friend in a different way. However, he didn't want to give her false hopes.

— I still love Tony girls.

— As long as I have a place in your heart, I'm happy, Tony said, sticking to him.

— You will always have a place in my heart.

They slipped under the duvet and fell asleep against each other. Tony squeezed his ass to keep Adrien's cum inside him and touched his cock one last time, as if to make sure he hadn't been dreaming, before closing his eyes. Adrien placed a kiss on those lips before turning off the light.

Boris Vian

After several hesitations, Adrien invited Rachel to have a drink in the "very particular" cocktail bar in Montmartre. He had never been there, but he thought the place would appeal to the Gothic. They were to meet there at the end of the morning.

Adrien presented himself in advance in order to locate the place. The floor was covered with black and white checkered tiles, heavy red armchairs and benches were available to customers. Many plants decorated the place creating a surprising and a little strange atmosphere. Behind the bar, a waiter offered cocktails with original recipes.

Adrien settled down in the glass roof among the plants. The place was amazing. We would never have thought we were in the heart of Paris.

Rachel arrived a little late. Dressed all in black with jeans, a sweater and a cardigan, she was also made up with dark trends. She also had a large purple shoulder bag. She sat down across from Adrien and smiled at him.

— Nice this place, I did not know.

— Neither do I.

— On the other hand, it will be difficult to fuck here. It's a shame taking a shot would have done me good, it's tense at the moment with my man. He's been painful since he came back from his shoot. He avoids me and barely touches me.

Adrien wanted to kiss Rachel and caress her small breasts. Gothic attracted him.

— We can go to my place.

— Next time with pleasure. Today it will be just poetry.

Adrien handed him the drinks menu. He had already studied it while waiting for her and was going to order himself the house cocktail. Rachel looked longingly at the different drinks before opting for a Mickey and Mallory Knox: Reposado tequila, five-spice stewed apple, house pommeau, lime and egg white.

— It's cool here, she said, putting the card down.

Adrien smiles: she also looked cool. She must have been a little older than him and had something mysterious that appealed to her.

— What did you think of Arthur Rimbaud's poems?

— It was good.

— I brought another author whom I like very much. Do you mind reading some verses?

— With pleasure.

Rachel took a book of poems by Boris Vian from her bag. Adrien knew the writer a little better than Rimbaud, he had read the foam for days.

"He was a real artist," Rachel said. At the same time poet, writer and musician. There is a lot of power in his words. Rachel started with "Why do I live".

> Why i live
> Why i live
> For the yellow leg
> Of a blonde woman
> Leaning against the wall
> Under the full sun
> For the round sail
> From a point of the port
> For the shade of the blinds
> Iced coffee
> That we drink from a tube
> To touch the sand
> See the bottom of the water
> That turns so blue
> That goes so low
> With fish
> The calm fish
> They graze the bottom
> Fly above
> Hair algae
> Like slow birds
> Like blue birds
> Why i live
> Because it's pretty

She continued with "Everything has been said a hundred times".

> Everything has been said a hundred times
> And much better than by me
> Also when I write verses
> Is that it amuses me
> Is that it amuses me
> It's just that it amuses me and I piss you off.

Rachel was reading in a sensual and engaged voice. She lived her text and gave off emotions as if each word came to life in her.

— It's powerful, said Adrien.

The waiter had brought them their cocktails. Rachel took a sip and caught her breath as if she had sweated all her soul to bring these worms to life.

— There is something strong in Vian, whether it is in these texts or in his music. He looked and went through his time seeing what was under the coat of varnish.

— He died young?

— Young and without having really known success. At the time, his books and poems were censored and commercial failures. Only music saved him. I see him as a living flay of his time. His song "the deserter" and his novel "I would spit on your graves" have been widely criticized.

— While today, he is recognized as an essential artist.

Rachel continued with the poem "life is like a tooth" before reading some quotes from Boris Vian.

Life is like a tooth At first we didn't think about it We just chewed And then it suddenly spoils It hurts you, and we hold on to it And we heal it and the worries And for us to be truly healed We need you snatch it, life

— He had a deep reflection on life and death. Listen to these quotes: "I don't know what is beautiful, but I know what I like and I find that more than enough"; "Pain is something that we have the right to inflict only on ourselves".

— It's beautiful, Adrien admitted.

— You should listen to his music, especially the jazz he played in the cellars of Saint Germain. There was a power in him when he played: as if life was coming out of his trumpet. His jazz transports me to another dimension. I have the impression of stepping back in time and sitting next to him in the cellar where he was playing.

— I'll listen to him, Adrien promised.

— It's a bit like this place, it feels like somewhere else, said Rachel, looking again at the decor of the very particular.

Buddha-bar style background music was played. Exotic green plants were arranged in each space of the canopy giving the impression of a jungle.

— I'm going to read you a last one that I appreciate That you are impatient.

Death passed that night,
To take a kid of fifteen,
To hug him in her big arms,
And suffocate her with her dress of hyacinths
Death slept that night

In a bed of a beautiful girl
For a once hug
And left only cold and scentless ash
That you are impatient, death
We make the way in front of you
It was enough to wait
That you are impatient, death
The lost game, you already know
All will start again
The sun on the water
You can't help it
Shadow of a flower
You can't help it
Joy in the street
Wild strawberries
A smile in May
You can't help it
A waltz waltz
You can't help it
A passing boat
You can't help it
A bird that sings
The grass of the ditch
And the rain so weary
You can't help it
Death returned tonight
With her dress of black irises
Death has returned to me
We knocked .. Open the door... There she is
She was burning like a lamp
In a night by the sea
She was burning like a red light
In the back of a deaf truck on the roads
How impatient you are, death ...

Even though the poem was about death, Adrien couldn't take his eyes off Rachel's lips. He wanted to kiss them even though they were painted black. He wanted to caress her pale skin, to take her in his arms to hug her. His gothic look hid wounds and flaws the depth of which he could not measure. Still, he wanted to lose himself in her.

— I love it when you read poems. I find you very beautiful.

— Thank you, said Rachel touched. Poetry is magic. In a few verses, a poem can overwhelm me and take me somewhere other than my starting point.

Rachel leaned over to Adrien and kissed him. Their kiss was sensual and romantic.

— I'm happy to know you, I feel good with you.

— Me too.

— I appreciate sharing these verses with you. My companion does not like poetry and makes fun of me when I read verses.

Adrien frowned. This man looked like an asshole who didn't take care of Rachel. He wondered what she found in him.

— We'll meet Again ?

— Yes and I still want to fuck with you. I would like now, but I have to go to work.

— That's when you want.

— I'll get back to you very soon.

They kissed again, finished their cocktail and left the very particular together, holding hands.

— Thank you for this moment, said Rachel

— Thank you to you for these beautiful poems and your company, said Adrien.

They made one last kiss in the street then they left each one on their side.

The rose petal

In the evening, Adrien met Tony at the apartment. They nibbled a quick bite in the kitchen, telling each other about their day.

— It was tight at the pizzeria. Como found out that Joey was cheating on him.

— How did he know?

— He saw a text message on Joey's cell phone and read their exchanges. It's been going on for months. Many of her absences to look for products for the pizzeria or to go to the bank were excuses to join her lover.

— How did Como react?

— He's devastated: he hasn't stopped telling me about it and plans to leave Joey for good this time. I feel sorry for him.

Adrien told him about his time spent with Rachel.

— You like her ? Tony asked.

— She's got something that touches me. She's not the prettiest I've had an affair with, but she's special.

— And in bed?

— Not even the best.

— Better than me ?

— No.

Tony then took a rose petal out of his shirt pocket. He had found it in a park which he had crossed to return to the apartment and had wanted to give it to her. It was red and yellow and very large.

— Thank you, said Adrien, kissing her on the mouth.

— You want us to do it again tonight?

Adrien hesitated: he had enjoyed fucking Tony, but he didn't want to do it again every night and risk falling into a relationship when he was his best friend. They were going to live together for a while and Adrien didn't want to risk damaging their friendship.

— I do not know, I hesitate. Is it okay to sleep with your best friend?

— I can just suck you off if you prefer.

Adrien loved it when his friend sucked him. Tony knew how to do it, more than Rachel or any other girl. He really wanted to be tempted. In his hand he held the rose petal that Tony had given him and he had the idea of offering his friend something else. Tony would bend over backwards to please her, he too could offer her something.

— How about I take care of your rose petal?

In surprise, Tony's eyes widened.

— My rose petal! Would you like to lick it for me?

— Why not. You always pump my cock, I could lick your ass for a change.

— I'm confused, Adrien. Few of my lovers have offered this to me. They prefer to bugger me and get off quickly.

Tony happily agreed and wanted to take a shower to clean his anus. The two boys went to the bathroom and undressed. Tony snuggled up to Adrien and kissed him.

— Thank you to you, it's great that you host me.

— It's normal, you're my best friend.

— I thought we had the best evening of my life, but now, I can't wait for you to take care of my rose petal.

They slipped into the tub and soaped themselves up. Tony insisted on his anus and even stuck a finger in it to rinse the inside. He unwound Adrien and gently cleaned his penis. Clean and dry, they went to Tony's room.

— Sit down, Adrien asked.

Tony lay down in the middle of the bed and spread his legs. Adrien got behind him and touched his little plump buttocks. He massaged them to warm them up then leaned over to lick them before moving smoothly towards Tony's asshole. He had only done this to one of his partners and wondered what his friend's reaction would be. He began to lick her anus and gradually push the tip of his tongue into it.

— Oh yes Adrien, it's good.

— You like it.

— Yes, continue.

Adrien then licked her anus with more force, thrusting his tongue as deep as he could in her ass. He also passed his hand under his friend and grabbed his penis stretched like an I. His cock was drooling on the sheets. With an energetic gesture, he began to jerk him off.

— Adrien, I won't be able to hold back for long.

— Drop everything.

Adrien activated for a moment longer on Tony's asshole while stroking his buttock with one hand and holding his penis with the other. He felt a rush of liquid flow through Tony's cock veins to spill over the bed.

— Ha! Tony cried, enjoying himself.

Adrien held his cock until all his cum drained out of him. Tony's body twitched several times. Adrien now had his fingers full of cum. On the bed, he stood next to Tony, whose eyes were filled with emotion.

— Thank you Adrien, it was great.

— I saw, my hand is wet, said Adrien tasting the sperm on his fingertips before his hand licked by Tony.

— It's very thoughtful of you to take care of my rose petal, Tony said, sticking to Adrien.

— It was a pleasure.

Tony watched Adrien's hard cock and decided he couldn't let it be. Adrien lay down on his back and Tony leaned over his crotch to take Adrien's cock in his mouth. He began by pumping her acorn while holding her penis. He then continued with a deep throat, putting all of Adrien's cock in his mouth, which Rachel had failed to do.

Excited to have licked Tony's ass, Adrien was not long to cum in the mouth of his friend who swallowed everything and licked his head to the last drop before snuggling up to him.

— That was great Tony.

— Soon you won't be able to do without it.

— I hope.

After lounging together for a moment, they decided to watch a monster movie on Netflix. Adrien went to put on a comfortable outfit in his room. Tony put on leggings and a pink sweater.

— Tomorrow, we'll watch football, there's the French team playing, said Adrien.

— No problem, you know I'm a fan of Giroux and Grizou.

Adrien went to get them two beers from the kitchen and as he walked back to the living room he heard the front door open.

Her face in tears, Ludivine entered crying. She seemed at wit's end as if her world had collapsed. Her make-up was just a memory, and her usually crisp clothes looked like a rag.

— Ludivine, what's happening to you? asked Adrien.

— I lost everything, she blurted out before bursting into tears.

Tony arrived and the two boys led him to the living room where Ludivine could not hold back her tears.

— It's horrible, horrible, she repeated between two sobs.

Adrien went to get her a glass of water to make her drink and try to calm her down.

Tony put his arm around her shoulders to console her. Ludivine was lost.

— I'm sorry I came here. I didn't know where to go. I will not disturb you, I will leave.

— No, you're not fit and you don't bother us, said Adrien. What is happening ?

It took a moment for him to speak.

— My future husband threw me out. We were supposed to visit a room in the suburbs for the wedding. I went to Maeva's to have an apricot waxed. He was waiting for me with Solène, my best friend, said Ludivine, sobbing. It was then that they told me that they had been sleeping together for months and that Solène was pregnant. He was going to take responsibility and marry her. He asked me to leave the apartment. Now he's going to live with Solène. As of tomorrow, I have to collect my things. He will wrap them up for me and put them on the landing. I don't even have any keys anymore, he took them back from me.

Adrien and Tony looked at each other in horror.

— This guy is a pig, Tony said angry.

— Never seen such an asshole, said Adrien scandalized.

— But I love him and I had to marry him. I had to start a family with him, have children...

Pissed off, Tony got up and lost his temper.

— It's monstrous what they did to you. They didn't deserve you.

— You're going to sleep here. We'll take care of you with Tony and tomorrow we'll go with you to collect your things.

Adrien and Tony tried to console Ludivine, but it was wasted effort. The young woman no longer knew where she was. She had been thrown out onto the street with just her purse and coat.

They made her drink a little alcohol to cloud her mind and led her to a bedroom where they slipped her into the sheets of the bed. Like a ghost, Ludivine let herself be guided.

— Try to sleep and don't hesitate to call us if you need to, said Adrien.

— Tomorrow we'll help you, Tony said.

They left the room leaving her alone with her grief.

— What an asshole this guy, Tony said.

— Poor thing, she doesn't deserve this.

The two boys promised to help him.

Ludivine's ex

In the middle of the morning, Adrien, Tony and Ludivine went to the old apartment of the young woman. Adrien had taken Viviane's car, a Mercedes class A in order to be able to take these things.

Ludivine looked like a zombie and seemed to be on autopilot. She didn't understand what was happening to her. She thought she was having a nightmare and was going to wake up. She hadn't closed her eyes all night and refused to swallow anything.

— It's not possible, it's not possible, she kept repeating.

Adrien and Tony didn't want to upset her and didn't know what to say to her to make her accept reality.

Adrien parked at the address indicated and they went up to the second floor of the building where on the landing many trash bags were piled up. Inside, Ludivine's clothes were loose. Panties were even on the floor.

— No that's not true. Why is he doing this? We have to get married.

— It's over Ludivine, said Adrien.

— But I love him.

— He's an asshole, Tony said, looking at the door to the apartment.

Ludivine dropped to the ground and started to cry again. Adrien and Tony started to load the car. In the street, Tony couldn't hold back his anger.

— What a bastard this guy, he said, looking up at the apartment.

Behind the window, a girl with long hair was watching them.

— It's coward what they did, said Adrien.

— They're assholes. She pains me Ludivine.

Leaning against the apartment door, Ludivine was crying and calling her friend.

— Marc, I'm here. Open up for me, I know you're here. There is your car in the street.

Adrien and Tony made a last round trip and came back to look for Ludivine.

— We must go, we loaded everything.

— No, no, I don't want to.

— It's finished Ludivine. We have to go, Tony said.

— And my stuffed animals. I don't have my fluff. I need my soft toys.

Tony then banged on the apartment door.

— Give Ludivine her soft toys. We know you are there.

Suddenly, the door opened. A burly, unshaven brunette appeared in front of them.

— Don't break my door, I'll give him his stuffed animals, he said glaring at Tony.

— Marc, I'm here, said Ludivine, but the man didn't glance at him.

He returned to the apartment and asked for a garbage bag from the woman with him. Ludivine did not dare to enter when she had lived here for years. From the entrance, Adrien and Tony observed the apartment. On the wall there were many frames with pictures of Ludivine's former companion posing in front of a convertible blue mini Cooper. The man brought the bag back and put it in front of Tony.

— Get out now.

A woman then appeared behind him.

— Solène, why? Why did you do this to me?

— I always got on well with Marc, better than you. It's better that way. You have to go now.

— But...

Tony grabbed Ludivine by the shoulders and led her with him.

— They are assholes, you have nothing more to do with them.

Adrien brought up the rear with the bag of stuffed animals. They slipped it into the car, but there wasn't enough room for one of them.

— It's Marc's mini, said Ludivine, pointing to the blue mini a few meters away.

— I want to break it, said Tony.

— They're looking at us out the window.

They made Ludivine climb to the front of the car and Tony gave a middle finger to Marc and Solène who were watching them from their window. Adrien entered the traffic and carried Ludivine away from the man she was to marry and from her ex-best friend.

For Ludivine

For three days, Ludivine remained locked in her room among the trash bags, refusing to eat. Attentive, Adrien and Tony tried to help him, but his mind seemed to have closed.

Adrien and Tony were watching a zombie movie when Ludivine reappeared in the living room. She was wearing the same clothes as when she arrived at the apartment in the middle of the night.

— I can't marry her anymore, she said, sitting down between the two boys. He's been cheating on me for months and laughing at me with the wedding. When I worked here, he slept with Solène.

— They are bastards. They didn't deserve you, Tony said, putting his arm around Ludivine.

— I must stink, it's been three days since I washed.

— You're chling," Tony confirmed, making them laugh.

Before Ludivine went to wash, Adrien asked her if she was hungry.

— I'm starving, I haven't eaten anything for three days.

Tony offered to give her some clothes as she hadn't unpacked her bags and Adrien went to the kitchen. A moment later, Ludivine joined them wearing loose gray jogging pants and a white t-shirt. Her blonde bob hair was wet.

A meal tray awaited him. She sat on the couch between Adrien and Tony and started to eat.

— My life is a disaster.

— It's a blow, Tony said. I've known a few, but never as violent as you.

Ludivine devoured her plate of pasta in a few minutes and Adrien served it again.

What are you watching ? Ludivine asked, seeing the television on pause.

— A zombie movie, you want us to change.

— No, I don't want to think about anything anymore.

Adrien poured her wine and between the two boys she tried for a moment to forget what had happened to her.

— There were sometimes misunderstandings between us, but I never imagined that.

— Do you feel like being alone for a few hours tonight? We have something to do with Adrien.

— I think I need to be alone.

— What do we have to do ? asked Adrien.

For two days, he had found that his friend had an odd attitude. He returned to the apartment with trash bags that he took to his room.

— You will see.

They took Ludivine to her room where they lined her up, then Tony asked Adrien to take the keys to the car. A few seconds later, they left the apartment with two garbage bags. They went to Ludivine's old apartment and parked two streets away.

— What do you want to do ?

— Avenge Ludivine. We're gonna break that asshole's cash register. I picked up dog poop. I'm going to rip the top of his car for him and empty everything inside for him.

— It's crazy !

— So what. He deserves it.

— You're right.

Like two criminals, they got out of the car and walked towards the mini. It was one in the morning and the streets were deserted.

Tony handed Adrien a cap and put one on as well. They quietly approached the car.

— Too bad, she is beautiful, said Adrien.

— Ludivine too. She didn't deserve this.

With a screwdriver, Tony tore the top off in several places as Adrien poured the bags of crap inside. Tony then taunted the body as Adrien kicked the mirrors and headlights at him. Carried away by their hatred, the two young men could no longer hold back. Tony smashed all four of his tires while Adrien, having found a cobblestone, smashed his windshield. Tony took pictures of their package before a light came on in a building window and they scampered like rabbits. They got back to their car and hurried away before bursting into laughter once the pressure dropped.

— I couldn't stop myself from hitting that box, said Adrien.

— This Marc pissed me off.

— I've never seen you like this.

The two friends decided to go for a drink to celebrate their revenge. Tony offered to go to the wizard, a lounge bar that did karaoke in the basement.

— I don't want to sing, warns Adrien.

They sat down at a table and ordered two beers from a local brewery. They needed that to get over their emotions.

— It will be hard for Ludivine, said Adrien.

— She hurts me, I like her, Tony said.

They chatted for a while until the three men at the table a little further away offered to join them.

— Then we can go to my place for a sex scene, one of them suggested.

— Not tonight, Tony said.

The men didn't insist and went back to their drink.

— It's hot in here, said Adrien.

— It's nothing, you've never been to a club with me.

— I'm not sure I like it, but if you want to go with them, I don't mind. I'll go home alone.

— I'm not going to leave Ludivine for a one-to-one sex plan and I already told you that I was in a relationship and very much in love.

They finished their beer and returned to the apartment.

•

When Ludivine got up, Adrien and Tony were already up. Tony pulled out his cell phone and showed her the pictures of the stoned mini.

— Did you do that? You are nuts!

— Doesn't that make you happy? Tony asked.

Ludivine looked at him and smiled, revealing her white teeth.

— It's done well for Marc. He was swelling me with his car. He will be furious when he sees this. Are you not going to be in trouble?

— Nobody saw us, said Adrien.

— You're great, said Ludivine, hugging them.

The notary

Two days later, Adrien went to see Edmond Delacroix, Viviane's notary, to talk to him about his aunt's property. Edmond, dressed in an impeccable charcoal gray suit, received him in his large office and offered him a coffee.

— I'm getting to know my aunt better. She's had a more eventful life than I imagined.

— Viviane was always on the move, going from one project to another.

Adrien told him about his meetings with the actors of the Libellule and Maeva troupe. He had also made the acquaintance of Giorgio, a restaurateur with whom Viviane was associated.

— I know them, said Edmond. I really like Pierre Labrume, we had a great evening together.

— You participated in the parties given by my aunt.

— I was very good friends with her, said Edmond knowingly.

Adrien then imagined Edmond having an orgy with the actors of the troupe. Beneath his reserved air, he hid his game well.

— What are my aunt's possessions? Ludivine also told me about properties abroad?

Edmond printed out a five-page list of real estate properties belonging to Viviane, then stood up and took a file out of a cupboard.

— Your aunt had created an offshore company in Delaware in order to lodge some capital there. This company is owned by another company in the Cayman Islands of which I am the administrator. With the capital withdrawn from the French tax authorities, she bought several luxury properties around the world. To maintain them, they are rented to wealthy vacationers. This is a great trail to start your journeys in the footsteps of your aunt.

— How many properties are there?

— Eight, but with the accumulated money, you can buy a ninth without difficulty. Here's the list, said Edmond, handing him a sheet.

The company was called Leguen Paradise. There was a villa in Mauritius, two properties in the United States, a Riad in Morocco, an apartment in the Cayman Islands, a property in Thailand, an apartment in Hong Kong, a property in Japan and another in Canada. .

— Your aunt had a knack for business. She turned everything she touched into gold and she knew how to choose her associates.

— How does this company work?

— The funds withdrawn were declared lost in foreign investments before reappearing in this offshore company which has several shell companies. They made it possible to buy the first property in Mauritius, then the system was self-sustaining. Without taxes or constraints, it is much easier to make a wealth grow.

— I really want to go to Mauritius.

Edmond checked on the internet that the villa was not rented and gave him the contact details of the agency that managed the property.

— Those who work there will be able to guide you during your stay there.

— It's not a sex and bed at least?

— A what ?

— Nothing, it's a joke.

— The villa is beautiful, I have been there several times.

They discussed Viviane for a while longer. Adrien now regretted not having been closer to her when she was still there.

— Is there a closed door in the apartment? I can't find the key. Do you know what's behind it?

— Yes, I know this room. I have a duplicate of the key. This is another side of Viviane. I advise you to open this door later, said Edmond, handing Adrien a key.

Adrien nodded and Edmond walked him back to his office door, advising him not to hang around for his graduation.

— I take care of it as soon as I come back from Mauritius.

departure

Back at the apartment, Adrien found Tony consoling Ludivine. The young woman was trying to regain her footing. A mug of tea in her hands, she had just cried. Her makeup had leaked.

— The rental agency called for you to agree to tenants, said Ludivine who had resumed her work to take care of the mind. It allowed him to stop thinking about his problems for a while.

Adrien told them about his interview with the lawyer.

— I decided to go to Mauritius first. You need to book three plane tickets.

— Three? asked Ludivine.

— One for Tony, one for you and one for me, for at least two weeks. I'm not going to go alone.

— Côme and Joey are going to bitch, but I'm not going to let such a great opportunity to leave for free. I am, said Tony, jumping for joy.

— Viviane never took me with her.

— I'm not Viviane and I need you.

— Thank you Adrien, said Ludivine moved.

Adrien couldn't leave her alone, especially in this state. He was starting to like her since he got to know her better.

— I don't even have a jersey, said Ludivine.

— We'll find you one over there. We're going to swim and eat lots of exotic fruits, Tony rejoices.

— I love fruit, said Ludivine.

— Is that why Maeva calls you her apricot? Adrien asked her to tease her.

— If you're nice, I'll show you my apricot, Ludivine promised.

End of the 1st volume

A word from the author

I hope you enjoyed Adrien's sexual adventures. Thus ends this first volume.

All the characters in this book were invented and any resemblance would be fortuitous.

Do not hesitate to leave me a comment, to tell me what you thought of it or to send me a little note (paulmail821@gmail.com).

I have a lot of fun writing these adventures and I hope you enjoy reading them.

I have also writing a winter romance MM: "Storm in Vermont".

With all my friendship.

Paul Mail

Contents

Adrien's sexual adventures ... 3

The beginning of the adventure ... 5

Cannes stay ... 13

Adrien's promise ... 23

Viviane's last wishes ... 31

The apartment ... 33

Ludivine, the assistant ... 37

Movie night ... 41

The invitation to the general ... 45

The Libellule theater ... 49

The two olives ... 55

The Mogai ... 59

Poetry under the roofs of Paris ... 63

A cafe at the Louvre ... 73

Tony's arrival ... 75

Ludivine and Tony ... 77

The first one ... 79

The evening with Tony ... 83

Boris Vian ... 89

The rose petal ... 95

Ludivine's ex 99

For Ludivine...101

The notary 105

departure... 107

A word from the author 109